The Viki...
Michael Mullen

Children's
POOLBEG

A Paperback Original
First published 1988 by
Poolbeg Press Ltd.
Knocksedan House,
Swords, Co. Dublin, Ireland.

ISBN I 85371 015 6

Cover design by Helen Pomphrey
Typeset by Print-Forme
62 Santry Close, Dublin 9.
Printed by The Guernsey Press Ltd.,
Vale, Guernsey, Channel Islands.

Also by Michael Mullen

For Teresa

Chapter One

 here was always the fear of Sitric. Even at night-time, protected by Ronan, Astrid feared this man of quick angers who ruled the city of Dublin. He was jealous of her lineage. In her veins she carried the royal blood of Ragnarr Lodbrok. There were many Vikings in the city of Dublin who wished that she were old enough to become queen and perhaps marry one of the princes of the O'Brians. It would bring security to the city. Alliance with the Leinster men had brought no peace. In the council chambers there had been divided opinions among the ship owners. They should make their peace with Brian Boru and submit to his tributes.

"This Sitric is dangerous," her father Ivarr often said when he returned from the councils. "He will bring destruction upon the city of

Dublin if he is given a free hand."

"He is low blood," Ronan the guard would add. "You should be king, Ivarr."

"His hatred for Brian makes him blind," Ivarr told them. "His mother Gormlaith, whispers in his ear. She is jealous of Brian Boru. It is this jealousy which could set all our ships on fire and destroy our city."

Ivarr was captain of a great ship and had many stories to tell them of his sea journeys to the south. The land was fertile and he could set up a trading post there.

"Why not take your fleet and find us a deep protected port and fertile land," Astrid often suggested, "Daily, Sitric gathers the pirates to himself, They band about him and insult us in the streets."

"Sitric and his slavers. They treat people less well than they do beasts," Ivarr said in anger. The slave pens were beside his warehouse at the river's edge. He had heard the slaves tearing at their chains, crying for water, while the pen keeper laughed at them and brought the whip lash down upon their backs.

"It is no longer a trading city," he often said, "but a mart for slaves. It is a city we should leave."

Ivarr often made this statement, but he never left the city. He was drawn to it by his ancestors who had sailed up the wide river and founded a trading post on the southern bank and fortified the hill above it with earthen walls and pallisades.

Ronan had been bought out of the slave pens. He would have fetched a high price had he not been wounded in the side by a Viking sword. When he reached the pens he had lost a large amount of blood. It was obvious to his captors that he would die. For two days he had lain in the corner groaning. He was a caged and wounded beast. In the deep pit, far away from his people and the woods and rivers, he would die. Two people entered the pits. He recalled the voice of Ivarr and the exchange of money. . .

He was taken to a house and placed on a pallet. Somebody spoke in Irish and told a servant woman to bind his wounds and encourage him to drink mead.

"He is thirsty and his lips are broken. He will perhaps die but at least he will be comfortable," a girl's voice said.

But Ronan refused to die. For ten days he lay in the large bed while a crust formed over the large wound on his side. He did not move or speak but slept for many hours. The servant, Orlaith, fed him with honey an gave him wine to drink. Strength returned to his body like the tide rising in a wide bay.

"Are you certain he will live?" a girl's voice asked Orlaith in Irish.

"He will. He has come back from the very jaws of death. Few are given the second gift of life."

Then one morning when Astrid looked down upon Ronan he was looking up at her, his eyes bright and blue. Ronan saw a girl of great beauty, whose fair hair fell down upon her shoulders and whose skin was white and rich like cream.

"You were very ill. You would have died but for Orlaith. She took great care of you."

"And what of your father? He brought me from the pens."

"Father is away. He sailed a week ago. He is carrying linen cloth and wool to the south."

Soon he was able to sit on a bench outside the house for an hour and look down upon the city. Looking north he could see Clontarf Island and the head of Howth like a wolfhound guarding the bay. Astrid had never seen such a huge man in her life. Ronan stood above all the other men and his shoulders touched the jams of the door when he entered.

There was much to observe from the bench outside the door. Astrid sat beside him and told him who the people were who passed by. Her most familiar friends were Gorm of the Crooked Nose, the Smith, and Sven of the Bent Back, the leather worker who had their shops nearby. They came and drank their wine and bread at mid-day, sitting on the long bench beside Ronan. He began to pick up individual words from them. Gorm of the Crooked Nose liked to fish from the pier which stretched out into the river. If the day were suitable, he would leave his work, take his hooks and line and spend it on the pier fishing. He talked to the traders and had all the news of distant places. Ronan often studied the smith as he worked out his designs on bone. They were his trial pieces as he called them and he had many square flat bones hanging from the beams of his shop from which his customers could select their designs.

"I'll have no truck with war," he often said, "and as for Sitric I'd have him banished from Dublin. He is only a trouble maker and a liar."

But he lowered his voice when the Leinster men passed by. They, like Sitric, would quickly draw their swords and enter a quarrel.

The city had been the scenes of many quarrels, particularly in the eastern quarter where Sitric himself lived.

From his seat he witnessed the slaves move past in sad procession to the pens where they would be auctioned or carried overseas, never again to return to Ireland. They bore frightened expressions on their faces and gazed in wonder at all the bustle about them.

Finally Ronan made his way to the market place. Here the traders had set up their stalls with their weighing scales and weights set out in front of them. They sold gold and silver bars by weight and ornaments by their artistic value. Elsewhere there were northern furs on sale which the women could sew up into warm cloaks. At other stalls one could buy rough goblets of wine and drink them under the canvas awnings and watch the crowd pass by. He had run his hands across fine cloth brought from the south. It was a strange city of many peoples. Once he had seen two merchants with skins yellow as whin, and on another occasion he saw a man with skin as black as a scribe's ink. Everywhere Sitric's men were to be seen. They carried the sign of Sitric upon them, the sign of the Black Raven.

"Carrion like their master," the merchants

said when they spoke amongst themselves. The forces of Sitric grew each year. Every malcontent and criminal was welcomed into his army. He was master of the slave trade and from this he drew his great wealth. When he appeared in the streets he was surrounded by six of his warriors, and men remained indoors until he passed. The merchants has to pay a tarrif to him in order to trade in the city and each year at special times they brought to him gifts of wine, gold and ornaments.

Orlaith said laughingly that Ronan ate more than three Vikings. She prepared large meals for him and watched in amazement as he ate them.

"You are the greatest eater in Dublin, Ronan," she said.

One day while Ronan and Astrid were in the market place they were approached by Knut, one of Sitric's men. He was wide-shouldered and low and often boasted of his great strength. He swaggered through the crowd and came face to face with Ronan. He was carrying a wine goblet in his hand. He was slightly drunk. He looked up at Ronan for a moment then dashed the contents of the cup into his face. The crowd looked on mutely at the arrogant display of Knut, who turned and walked away.

Anger surged through Ronan. He summoned up the strength within him. Heedless of any consequence he rushed after the retreating figure. He caught Knut by the back of his meshed jerkin and the seat of his leather trousers and lifted him above his head.

"Let me down, you brute. Let me down," Knut cried.

Ronan carried him to the quayside followed by the crowd. He stood for a moment, then spun him around several times. Finally he threw Knut into the river. He fell into the water. When he surfaced he cried out, "Save me I cannot swim. My armour will carry me to the bottom."

Ronan did not wait to see Sitric's men cast a line to him. He turned and walked through the crowd. He felt weary. He had over-exerted his strength and he feared that the wound had opened. His side pained him. Meanwhile Astrid had rushed home to Orlaith and told her all that had happened.

"Ivarr will not like this at all," she kept muttering. "He does not wish to tangle with Sitric."

Ronan was pale when he reached the door of the house.

"Let me see the wound," Orlaith told him. He lifted his jerkin. The upper part of the wound, had broken and was bleeding.

"You are lucky," she said. "You will have to rest for several days. You did a foolish thing."

"I did not," he said. "I will not have Sitric's men cast the dregs of wine cups into my face."

"Don't abuse him, Orlaith," Astrid said, "Knut insulted him. He was right to do what he did."

"You are as bad as he is. Wait until your father comes home and I shall tell him about the way you run about the stalls and take Ronan down dangerous alleyways."

Next day he sat on the bench in the front of the house and gazed down at the city. Little did he know that the news of the incident had passed quickly through all the streets of the Norse town. Many said that Ronan had the strength of two oxen. Others stated that it seemed some strange power took control of his body and that he was possessed. No warrior except the Black Warrior had such strength. Gorm of the Crooked Nose came and sat beside him on the long bench.

"I am very proud of you, Ronan. You have done our quarter a great service. Sitric's men will mind their manners when they enter here in the future.

We hear that Knut is in disgrace. Sitric has had harsh words with him and he is no longer a leader among his men."

"How do you know all these things?" Ronan asked.

"News travels quickly in Dublin. A story goes across the town and back again in a half day. We drank to your health at the pot house last night." He cut out his design on the flat surface of a bone as he spoke.

"Do you possess a sword, Ronan?" Gorm of the Crooked Nose asked.

"No. I lost my sword when I was captured. It was too small for me. I had little training in the art of sword play."

"Well then you shall have a proper sword. I shall forge it for you myself and place your mark upon it. And Sven of the Bent Back will make you a scabbard. But you must have some training."

"Who will teach me?" Ronan asked.

"I shall teach you, for not only can I make swords but I know the art of sword play."

"Will it be a large sword?"

"The largest sword in Dublin."

Ronan was tired that evening when he went indoors and fell into a heavy sleep. But that night Gorm of the Crooked Nose did not sleep. He called his friend Gruder the ring maker. He was an old man. On many occasions he had been subjected to abuse from Sitric's men, who demanded tributes of gold.

"Let us forge a sword for Ronan," he told him. "While the city sleeps. He is our best protector."

"Oh I have heard great stories about him," Gruder said.

They went into the shop of Gorm of the Crooked Nose. Behind his shop he had his smithy. It was a dark place with a hugh leather bellows and snout. There were a few small coals among the embers which Gruder raked together. Soon they had a bright fire burning. Gorm of the Crooked Nose opened a large chest and took out a leather satchel. Carefully he undid it and revealed the blade of a large sword.

"Is it Frankish?" Gruder asked.

"Yes, smuggled out of France many years ago. Made in the monastery forges there. None better you know," said Gorm of the Crooked Nose.

"Then it is of great value," Gruder said.

"I care not for it's value. I have hidden it for many years waiting for a proper owner. Now I have found one." Gruder looked at the sword blade with an expert eye. "Best swords ever made, these Frankish swords. It is broad and flat and has a grooved blade."

All night they worked in the forge, Gruder pulling on the bellows. They talked about the city business and the latest gossip. But always they returned to the subject of Sitric and his ambitions to rule all Ireland.

"He is a dangerous fellow and will come to no good." At the darkest hour of the night when the city was well asleep they broke from their work and drank wine. It was cool and red. Binding the hilt to the main body of the sword was a delicate task. The strength and the weakness of the sword depended upon this. When the cocks were crowing in the eastern quarter of the city the task was done.

They slipped out of the shop by the back alley and called upon the leather worker, Sven of the Bent Back. He took the sword in his hand and tested the balance of the weapon.

"It is perfect. The blade is large and the hilt strong. I have the perfect scabbard and belt for it." He brought them into the back of his shop and took down a scabbard of strong leather, embossed with writhing figures and tipped with silver at the base. The sword slid evenly into the scabbard.

"They were meant for one another. Who is this sword for?" Sven of the Bent Back asked.

"Ronan. He will need it to protect himself from Sitric's men and from Sitric himself."

They spoke for some time in the small room behind the shop. It was almost mid-day when they made their way up the hill to Ivarr's house. Ronan was sitting on the long bench.

"We have a gift for you, Ronan," they said directly.

"A gift . Why do I deserve a gift?"

"Because we think, Ronan, that it is suited to you. None other is worthy of such a gift."

And with that Gorm of the Crooked Nose took the scabbard bearing the sword from beneath his cloak. Gorm of the Crooked Nose held it in both hands and offered it to him.

"I am unworthy of such a gift," he said.

"Take it," they urged. "Draw the sword from the scabbard and see if it suits you."

Ronan took the scabbard gently and looked at the ornaments running down each side. He grasped the sword handle and drew away the sword. It was a magnificent object, precious because of the gold inlay, strong because its blade was forged in a Frankish monastery. When he felt it in his hand he knew that this sword was created only for him.

"Test it," Gorm of the Crooked Nose urged. He stood up and cut at the air. It was alive in his hand and part of him.

"I need fine training to use such a sword."

"I shall train you. I shall train you," Gorm of the Crooked Nose said, delight growing in his eyes.

In the weeks which followed Gorm of the Crooked Nose abandoned his business and he was not seen fishing on the quayside. Instead he spent the time in the enclosure of Ivarr's house. He made a dummy of straw and sacking which he suspended from a beam. With the aid of this dummy he trained Ronan, showing him side strokes, body strokes and strokes to the head. His small figure became very fierce as he charged at the dummy and attacked it.

"This is very serious," he would tell Astrid when she laughed at him.

As Ronan's strength improved so did his sword skill. He engaged in sword play with Gorm of the Crooked Nose until he knew the Viking skills.

"These are the old skills I teach you. Each day you must spend a long time in practice, And always remember the body movements.

They must be agile."

Ivarr's journey to the south lasted six months. One day Astrid sighted his sail entering the bay.

"Father is home," she cried with delight. "He is safe." She put on her long white dress, which was drawn about her waist by a leather belt and clasped with a silver buckle, and placed her fur cloak upon her shoulders. She went with Ronan down the hill to the quayside.

Ronan, his sword in his scabbard, stood beside the Princess on the long wooden quay and observed the ship approach. It was smooth timbered and moved easily over the waters. It stood out amongst all the other ships as a splendid craft. At the prow stood Ivarr, his arms and face tanned by the southern sun, his body trim. He waved to them from the centre of the river, he found a berthing place and secured the ship to the pier. When he set foot on the quay Astrid rushed to and jumped into his outstretched arms.

"And how is my Princess?" he asked.

"Well," she replied. "I have so many stories to tell."

"And I have many stories to tell you. Stories which will make you eyes widen in wonder, for

I have visited the city of Constantine, I have brought you gifts of perfume and silks from beyond the sandy wastes."

Hand in hand they walked along to where Ronan stood by himself. As they approached, Ivarr studied his appearance. He did not realise that he was such a huge man. His face had lost its unhealthy palor. He looked at the sword by his side and wondered how he had obtained it. Clearly he was confident of himself and knew his way about the quays.

"I did not know what to expect when I returned," Ivarr said. "I find a trim soldier, healthy and strong."

Ivarr had made a prosperous voyage. He had sailed on to the farthest city and returned with precious cloth, jewels and wine. That night he held a feast for the men who had ventured upon the unknown seas with him. Many of them were blood relations who would as quickly take up the sword in his defence as sail with him. He paid them in sound coinage and in gold and then they sat at the long table and drank mead and ate fine meats. It was a night of gaiety and stories. Ivarr told of their adventures upon the high seas. Time passed pleasantly and they did not notice the morning light fill the sky.

Chapter Two

itric, son of Olaf Cuaran and Gormflait of Leinster, carried Norse and Irish blood in his veins. He had spent many summers at Naas of the kings and it was here that he had hunted boar with his uncle Maelmorda. Dublin was a day's distance from Naas of the Kings. The journey lay across open flat land, broken by woods and forests. The enemies of Sitric and Maelmorda lay to the west and the north. The pleasant lands of Leinster held no fears for Sitric.

He had a deep and lasting hatred of Brian Boru which had been nurtured by his mother and his uncle.

"Watch the Dail Gash," she told the war lords of Leinster. "They are made from tough fibre. They have adopted the Viking armour and war tactics."

"They will be beaten back to their barren limestone land from which they had emerged," the others argued. But in 968 Brian's brother Mahon defeated the Norwegian King of Limerick and plundered the city. A new force was appearing in Munster more ferocious than the Vikings themselves. The kings of Leinster began to fear this new power from the west.

"Mahon will over run us," they said in their councils. "We must make peace with him."

But Mahon died and his place was taken by his younger brother Brian.

"Perhaps he is weak and will not retain the lands of Munster and the crown of Cashel," they said of the new leader. They misjudged him. He bound the tribes together and held Munster.

"He will defeat us if you do not move on him. Move before he grows too powerful," Gormflaith had advised. They did not move quickly enough.

*   *   *

Olaf Curan died and Sitric became king of Dublin. Many said that Ivarr should have been king. He had pure Norse blood in his veins; he was balanced in his judgments and he was friendly with Brian of Munster. Sitric worried about Ivarr. And he was jealous too of Astrid. Some day Ivarr would produce the Nordic Crown and the people would flock to his banner. Ivarr would be declared king and his daughter would succeed him. "The Nordic crown does not exist," his mother had told him. "You fret too much about it."

"It does," he said. "Ivarr knows of its existence, With that crown he could claim the throne."

"Then why has he not produced it before now?" she asked.

"Because he bides his time. He will wait until I am weak and in disgrace. Then he will claim it."

"You are too suspicious," she said.

"I learned my suspicion from you. You taught me not to trust anybody."

During Sitric's reign Dublin became a city famous only for its trade in slaves.

And while the city lost its power Brian Boru built up his army. He became known throughout Munster for his wisdom, for his interest in learning and for the restoration of the monasteries and the churches.

And then Brian turned his attentions

towards Leinster. He would subdue this rich territory. Quickly Maelmorda and Sitric marshalled their forces.

"We will settle the old scores with this upstart from Munster," they pledged as they toasted each other in wine before the battle. But Brian trapped them in Glen Mama. They turned to flee only to find their retreat cut off. Maelmorda had taken refuge in a yew tree and hid amongst its leaves. Brian's son, Murchad, had dragged him with a rope about his neck to Brian's camp. Kneeling before Brian he promised to pay yearly tribute to him. Brian spared his life and let him return to his kingdom, a mistake he was later to regret.

Sitric made his way back to Dublin, his men dispossessed of their arms. They returned at night-time so that no one would witness their humiliation. He must now pay tribute to Brian, and to make matters worse his mother married Brian. She saw in Brian a future King of Ireland. She would become Queen of Ireland.

Gormflaith urged Brian to move forward swiftly. She was forever pressing him to move into the north and she wished to join the councils of war.

"Is there no end to your ambition?" Brian asked her. "You meddle in my affairs. One moves only from certainty."

"You will grow old and never become High King," she said. "Your troops are ready to move on Malachy and you have the backing of Leinster and yet you bide your time."

"I will move when the time is ripe. I have fortresses to build and roads to repair between the kingdoms. The books have to be restored. You think only of war and conquest."

He would have tolerated her arguments and her ambitions. However, she began to interfere with his sons, setting one against the other. Murchad, Connor and Flann each in turn were told that Brian favoured them. They would succeed when he died. It was his adviser the monk Lorcan who told him of the divisions in his family.

"She is a serpent sent to divide your kingsmen," he said boldly to Brian when he visited the monastery at Killaloe.

"What shall I do Lorcan?" he asked.

"Send her back to Leinster. When we have our divisions healed let her return again. You wish to be Emperor of the Irish, like Caesar was Emperor of Rome and Charlemange Emporer of the Holy Roman Empire. Well,

Gormflaith will destroy the plans you have made."

Brian did not immediately take his advice. Of all the women of Ireland Gormflaith was the most beautiful and the most intelligent. She would not sit among the women and she would not hold her tongue. She continued her intrigues.

"She will be another Maeve," Lorcan warned him. Brian had drawn her aside and told her of the accusations made against her.

"Let me see my accusers. Let me see them. They spin lies against Gormflaith. I have only the interests of the great Brian at heart."

Brian believed her. But then Lorcan, who had made his way post haste from Killaloe, asked for a private meeting with him. He carried with him several sheaves of parchment. They were the copies of letters which had passed between Gormflaith and her brother Maelmorda. She had betrayed the secrets of his kingdom to her brother.

"She is set upon destroying our kingdom," Brian said when he examined them.

"Yes," Lorcan said directly.

"But are they genuine?"

"They are."

"Can I trust your judgment in these

matters?" Brian asked.

"You must, I cannot tell you how they came into my hands but I received them from a monastery close to Naas of the Kings."

The next meeting between Brian and Gormflaith was a painful one.

"I will see that you get safe passage through my territories. I will send my best soldiers to protect you. Take the gifts you carried to this fortress and bring also your servant women. You have betrayed my confidence. You may return to this dun once every year if you so wish to see your son Donnchad. Do not meddle in my affairs again."

"You will never be High King now. Had you followed my advice it would have been so. There will be battle between us some day, Brian of the Tributes. The writers of the annals will speak highly in my favour."

Brain stood later in the tower of his palace and watched the cavalcade move eastwards.

She had the mind of a great leader, the heart of a soldier but the impatience of a woman, Brian observed as he watched her move away. He looked down at the wide fortress he had built. It would be a lonely place without her.

For Sitric, his mother's move back to

Leinster was a welcome event. Her ambition now was to destroy Brian.

But Sitric's chance of revenge did not immediately arise. It was obvious to Ivarr that Brian Boru with his powerful army, his firm rule, could unite Ireland. He was not surprised when in 1002 Brian moved towards Meath with a powerful army. Malachy had a month to prepare for battle but when he saw Brian's troops in the field he withdrew from battle, and Brian Boru became King of Ireland. Brian was now supreme ruler and when he inscribed his name on the Book of Armagh he added the words "Emperor of the Irish."

On hearing the news, Sitric retired to the pagan grove in the east of the city, sacrificed an animal to the gods, and offering a cup of blood to a graven image promised that he would yet destroy the usurper. He prayed to the pagan dieties that the reign of Brian would be short-lived, that the soft god of the Christians would be destroyed and that he, Sitric would become master of all the great ports and sea routes.

Chapter Three

rian Boru, on summer evenings, looking from his dun across the landscape of Clare, felt battle weary and old. His faithful scribe Lorcan was often at his side ready to inscribe on parchment the account of his battles and his reign. It would all be set down in the Book of Clare when Brian died.

"Tell me Lorcan, what is your greatest wish?" Brian asked one evening as they sat by his small tent set above the wide and tranquil river Shannon.

"My wish, noble Brian, is to build a small cell of wattle and clay on Lough Derg and end my days in peace."

Lorcan had been with them many years and second only to Brian himself knew the secrets of the kingdom.

"I cannot do without you, Lorcan. You alone

I can trust and you alone know the workings of my mind."

"Too well I know the workings of your mind. For you the country is like a chess game, the petty chief's pawns, the great chief's larger pieces."

Brian now in his seventy-fourth year was beginning to take life easy. It was time for both of them to hand over power to the younger men. But who could take his place? His son Murchad had a violent temper and an unrestrained tongue, Connor was wise but not a war leader. Flann had the best qualities for leader. But perhaps his people would look outside his family and choose another leader. There was always the danger that they might begin to fight amongst themselves and that would give his enemies the chance they needed. What had been built with care could be easily and quickly destroyed.

Their minds were drawn from the affairs of state by the approach of a long ship. It had Brian's mark upon the wide sail. From prow to stern it was graceful of line as it moved across the calm waters of Lough Derg. About the mast the weather vane caught the wind directions. A strong voice called out directions and the yard carrying the sail swung to catch the wind.

"They manage the ship with great ease these sailors of yours," Lorcan commented.

"Well, they ought to. They have been trained by the very Norse themselves. The masts were brought from the forests of Leinster. When I look at these ships sail by I remember that it was Maelmorda of Leinster that carried them here over many miles. It galls Maelmorda to carry the tribute," Brian told Lorcan.

"He is the one to fear of all others," Lorcan said.

"I know. The weakness of the country lies in Leinster. However, for eleven years I have held the country together."

It had been a golden summer. The berries were red on the rowan trees, the apples bent the branches upon the trees. The honey in the hives was already golden and full. About them the scent of flowers was heavy and sleep-inducing.

"I will rest now in my tent, Lorcan. I am afraid I am giving way to old age. In my youth I never slept but moved constantly through the woods of Munster bearing down upon Lochlann's stronghold in evening time. I feel age heavy upon me."

Lorcan beckoned a young giolla who was grazing Brian's horse close at hand. He rushed to the tent, opened it and then arranged the lamb skins, white as milk, on the framed bed. This bed was a gift from Ivarr of Dublin. He had written to Brian that in his old age he should enjoy such comforts.

"You coddle me like a child," Brian told Lorcan. "I have slept upon damp moss, green rushes and young branches."

"And it is because of that that your bones ache in the winter weather and that you have to lie in the sweat house."

"Leave me be. I can still walk and drink my wine," he told them stubbornly.

Lorcan noticed that the years and the old wounds were taking their toil upon Brian. He limped heavily when he walked, his head was low upon his shoulders, his back arched. The beard was stranded with greys and whites. But his mind was sharp as a sword edge, his eyes bright like rich stones. Nothing escaped his attention.

He sat upon the edge of the bed for a moment then he eased himself on to the lamb skins. Lorcan stood by the bed for some time. When Brian had fallen asleep he left the tent and closed the flap. Then he signalled to the woods. Several soldiers who had been hiding there emerged, arms at the ready. They stood about the tent protecting it from the sudden attack by an enemy. Those who feared the challenge of Brian in the field had sent their assassins into Brian Boru's territory. Brian was never aware of this protection. He was always careless of his personal safety and it fell to Lorcan to insure that he was guarded at all times.

Lorcan lay on the grassy slope and left aside his parchment quill and ink horn which he always carried about with such fuss. Like Brian, he too was growing old. He felt the summer heat about him. Soon he was asleep. He had a recurring dream. Brian had finally set him free from his work at the court. He could at last set our for the lonely island in Lough Derg. With a wind from the south following, he hoisted the sail of his small boat and moved away from the shipyards where Brian built ships and the forges where the smiths made the arms for war and the circular shields. The sun had flushed the sky with graded colours, the air was filled with evening bird song, the waters about him silk-fine as he made his way to the lonely island where he would have a few years to himself. It was always the same dream and it varied little. It was a dream with colours rich as the illuminated manuscripts. While he slept dreaming of evening, the mid-day passes. The giolla shook him awake. He snapped out of sleep, made the landscape about him firm and went to waken Brian. By this time his grandson had caught three salmon and had moved farther down the bank of the river.

The heat was not now intense. A small breeze shook the fine material of the tent. Brian came and sat upon his throne. The giolla brought a goblet of red wine and then retired to a suitable distance.

"You slept too, Lorcan," Brian said after he had sipped their wine.

"Yes, my Lord Brian. I succumbed to the heat of the day."

"Oh no you did not. Like me you succumbed to old age. Some day I must free you from my service and let you go to this island of yours."

This was that part of the day when Brian dictated his letters.

"And to whom shall you write to today, Brian? Many people call out for letters."

"I must write to my good ally Ivarr. Of all the Norse men I trust him most of all. He came with me to Tara. He understands my mind."

"What shall I say to him?"

"Wish him well. And invite his daughter Astrid to Kincorca with her bodyguard, Ronan. It is a year since she visited me. My ship will meet her at the upper lake and bring her here."

Lorcan quickly inscribed the letter. Then Brian took the quill and put his name to it.

"I hope she accepts the invitation to Kincora. I have a special interest in her. She has the best qualities of her race and will grow into a fine woman. Perhaps she might one day marry a high king of Ireland and the marriage put the seal of peace between the Lochlanns and the Gael."

"And what of Sitric?" Lorcan asked.

"I would banish him. I know his dangerous nature."

"He will turn upon you Brian."

"Not yet. He cannot because he has not the power. He could of course bring in Maelmorda with him, but without outside support he would not equal me in the field."

"The Lochlanns are stirring. Across the Irish sea they have attacked the towns of Britain. They are in fever again."

"If that danger arises there will be a final battle. I have fought twenty times with them.

They know that I am equal to them. There is little chance of this final battle. The fever as you call it will pass."

"And tell me Brian, does the Nordic crown exist? They say that if Ivarr produced this crown Sitric would be banished by his own people."

Brian thought for a while and milked his grey and white beard. He looked reflectively at the river passing slowly and majestically by.

"You know all my secrets, Lorcan. Why should I keep the final secret from you. The crown does exist. Only Ivarr and I know where it lies hidden. I can tell you no more."

And with that he fell silent. Lorcan did not ask any more questions.

"Make sure the letter is dispatched to Dublin as soon as possible. If Astrid comes she should come in late summer or early autumn when the roads are passable."

Brian dictated four letters. Then with a gesture of his hand he signalled that he was weary of the affairs of state. Lorcan left aside the parchments and set out the gold and silver chessmen on the chessboard.

"What shall we wager?" Brian asked.

"Your kingship of Ireland against my island

in Lough Derg."

"Very well then."

They turned their attention to the gold and silver figures on the chessboard. Each move was calculated with care. Behind them the sun began to set. Slowly the sky filled with saffron and later dull red.

"You are a wily scribe," Brian said when Lorcan made a good move. For Brian the chessboard was a battlefield, for the scribe it was an enchanted wood. Darkness came and the giolla brought two torches. The soldiers moved down from the forest and formed a circle about the figure of Brian and the Scribe. The night wind was velvet soft about them. And finally, with the moon bright in the east and the Shannon a road of gold, Lorcan made the master move.

"I have beaten Brian," he laughed. "I have won the kingdom of Ireland."

The soldiers folded the camp and the giolla brought Brian's favourite horse up from the river meadow. Lit by torches, Brian and his retinue made their way to his fortress at Kincora.

Chapter Four

ith the passage of time Ronan began to understand and then to speak Norse. He could now move freely through the streets which were never without interest.

Dublin was a city of soldiers, sailors and merchants. The merchants lived close to the quays in Wine Street, Gold Street, Silk Street and other streets called after their trades. They were cautious men and had soldiers in their employment to protect them from thieves and rogues who lived in the district called The Warren. This was a filthy place of innumerable twisting streets and alleyways, with beer houses and wine taverns of a low order. The merchants were men with soft hands and soft faces. They had contacts in cities as far away as Constantinople and

Novgorod.

Sitric's quarter was on the eastern limits of the city and bound by marshes. Here Sitric worshipped the pagan god Odin. It was rumoured that each year slaves were sacrificed to placate Sitric's god and that their bodies were hung from trees about a rough temple.

Ronan was now guardian to Astrid. They often rode together south. They brought with them food parcelled by Orlaith. Their destination was the mountain of the three rocks. From here they could see the city of Dublin and the ships at sea. Sometimes they ventured deeper into the mountains but there was always the danger from robbers. At other times they crossed the river at the bridge and made their way along Clontarf strand to Howth. In the evenings as they returned home, they races along the wide and spacious beach. In the bay stood an island, rising gently out of the water. Here among the hillocks tufted with marram grass lived a colony of rabbits, which provided some food for many of the small settlements close to the shore. To the west was Tomar's Wood and the well of the Saint.

Astrid was an expert horsewoman. Her first

gift from her father had been a pony and at twelve she could ride a spirited horse. On horseback she feared no danger, taking fences and streams in an easy manner, her blonde hair flying behind her in the wind.

Ronan was now a familiar sight in the streets and alleyways of Dublin, feared for his great strength and the sword which he carried by his side. It was doubted by many if Ronan's swordplay equalled his strength.

"He is a swordsman by default," Sitric often said to his men. "He has not been tested in single combat."

"Send a man to challenge him, Sitric," they told him. "To defeat and kill Ronan on a single combat would be to weaken the power of Ivarr. And humiliate him among his followers in the eastern quarter."

A challenge was sent to Ronan and delivered openly in front of Ivarr's house. Twice the challenge was issued until Orlaith threw a pail of water upon Sitric's minion.

"Go away," she called to him. "Leave decent people sleep. We want none of Sitric's cocks here heralding in a false dawn. Away with you back to your quarter."

Rumours began to circulate in the western quarter that Ronan was a coward, a large child with great strength and no courage.

"Ronan is a large child," they said to each other when they met in the alleyways.

"And soft too."

"Three times the challenge has been made to him and three times he has refused."

"Ivarr's man like Ivarr himself is soft. Sitric's men have returned to our quarter demanding heavy tribute from the merchants."

The merchants complained that Ivarr was no longer the soldier who marched with Brian Boru to Clontarf to wrest the crown from Malachy. The western quarter became nervous, man spoke in whispers, the traders wondered if Sitric would slaughter them and seize their wealth. One cautious merchant folded his stall, put his jewels and gold into a large coffer and sailed out of Dublin.

"I will not have you expose your life in the Pit," Ivarr told Ronan. "The Pit is a savage place. There they fight to the death. I have seen slaves savaged by dogs there while men cast wagers. I have seen slave set against slave to entertain drunken soldiers."

"Then I am to be called a coward, Ivarr," Ronan said.

"Yes, let them call you a coward. Let them

call you a coward."

"And have children mock me in the streets?"

"Yes. That is Sitric's doing. He wishes to strike at me through you."

"You place a hard burden upon me."

"I know."

Ronan fell silent. He was angry with Ivarr but he owed him his life and would not challenge his authority. However, his kingsmen complained.

"Sitric's men are back in the quarter. They detect weakness of purpose amongst us. Sitric struts like a cock through Dublin. claiming that he is overlord, saying that he will destroy Brian's puppet."

"Ronan will not fight in the Pit. Let there be an end to the matter," Ivarr told them.

They did not speak of Sitric in Ivarr's household. Yet the whole city knew what had taken place at the counsel house. Sitric was certain that Ivarr was losing his sharp edge for battle. He was growing old and growing comfortable. He directed his men to move further into Ivarr's quarter and to harrass the merchants and demand heavier tribute from them. They pushed Ivarr's men aside and hurled insults at Ronan as they passed the house.

"Astrid, what shall I do?" Ronan asked as they sat outside the house and suffered the insults.

"Challenge them. You have secretly practised with the sword for three years. Gorm of the Crooked Nose thinks that you can beat off any opponent. You must stand and fight."

Her voice was firm. He looked at her face. Her eyes were flashing with anger.

"You know what they say of the Pit, Astrid. Two men enter and one returns. In the Pit they fight to the death."

"I would not have you die, Ronan," she said.

"I have been very close to death. I do not fear it. I have been given the gift of life a second time and I must use it well. I must think deeply concerning this matter."

Ronan walked by the quays taking no heed of the graceful ships secured to the wooden jetties or the movements of goods from store to ship and ship to store. He heard only the babble of voices coming to him in a half-sleep. Ivarr did him an injustice not to let him accept the challenge. He moved away from the quay and made his way behind the stores to the slave pens. They were heavy circular pallisades guarded by Sitric's soldiers. Slavers from the east moved from pen to pen examining the slaves, complaining about their weakness and ill health, haggling over the price. It was a sad world over which he had no control. The sound of the slave world through which he was passing was familiar to him. He stopped his ears to the voices which pleaded through the small slits in the large wooden stakes. And then he heard a voice out of the past. It was the voice of his dead sister.

"Ronan, Ronan," the voice called out again. "It is I, your sister Aisling."

He cleared his mind of his angers and looked about him. The voice came from one of the pens close by. He rushed to the small slit between the timbers and pressed his eye as close as he could. Within the enclosure he recognised his sister and his two brothers. They had ropes about their necks and were secured to timber posts driven in the ground. They were hungry and tired, their tunics torn and dirty. He looked at Aisling. Her long dark hair was dishevelled, her eyes were filled with fear. He called out to them.

"Aisling, Sean, Tadgh. I thought you were dead these three years. The dun was put to the torch and I was told none survived."

"While you fought many of us fled to the

woods, Ronan. We lived there for many days on nuts and berries. We never returned to the dun but were captured by Darach who ill-used us for many years and now we find ourselves in this strange place. Save us Ronan. Save us from slavery. We are the only survivors of the terrible slayings."

"If I should die in the attempt I shall save you. You shall be free again. You shall return to your dun rich in ornaments and fine clothes."

Summoning his great strength which had lain dormant for so long he grasped two of the wooden stakes and began to shake them. Waves of blind fury surged through him and he would have torn down the pallisade had not ten of Sitric's soldiers surrounded him. They drew their swords as they approached.

Aisling cried out, "The soldiers gather about you." Ronan moved quickly around and watched the circle of swords close in upon him. Gorm of the Crooked Nose had trained him well. He flicked his sword upward out of his scabbard and caught the hilt as it passed down in front of him. The attention of the soldiers was drawn to the movement. When they gazed again at Ronan, he held the sword double handed in front of him. Such was his fury that he could have hacked them to pieces. Then a voice of caution spoke in his mind.

"Sitric has issued a challenge three times to me. Tell him now that I accept it. Let him send his mightiest warrior to the Pit against me. If I win then I seek as a prize the three slaves of this pen. Bring this message to Sitric," he said.

"Then you will leave the pallisade secure?" one of the soldiers said.

"The pallisade will remain secure."

With this guarantee they sheathed their swords and Ronan moved away from his position. One of the soldiers mounted his horse and rushed through the streets and lanes towards the quarter of Sitric calling out.

"Ronan has accepted Sitric's challenge. Ronan has accepted Sitric's challenge."

Ronan immediately went to the market place where he purchased food and warm clothing for his sister and brothers. He bribed the guard to allow him enter the pen. Their meeting lasted only a little while. Ronan assured them that he would return and set them free.

The city was seething with excitement. Already the news had spread through all the streets and alleyways. The merchants talked about it to their customers. In the taverns and the beer dens bets were placed.

"Sitric's man will win. Who would place a bet upon an unknown and untested fool?" many of them commented scornfully.

Others hesitated in their bets. This fool, as they called him, had exceptional strength. Even if his swordsmanship was faulty his strength made the contest even. The odds were good. For one gold piece they could win three. They bet their gold pieces on the off chance that Ronan would win. The commerce of the city was disrupted.

When Gorm of the Crooked Nose and Sven of the Bent Back heard the odds they rushed down to the tavern and bet ten gold pieces each on Ronan. They then rushed back to Gorm's small shop, took down a dusty jar of wine and poured themselves two large goblets. Their hands shook with excitement.

"This is the moment we have trained him for," they said to each other.

"Yes," they agreed and rushed to another tavern and placed ten more gold pieces on Ronan. They returned and drank more wine.

"You know," Gorm of the Crooked Nose said while they supped their third glass of wine. "If Ronan is defeated then we will have to flee the city. I have placed all my tribute money upon him."

Astrid rushed into the small shop.

"Ronan is coming up the hill now. Father is in a fury. He says that Ronan will destroy him. Come quickly, come quickly."

Uncertain of their steps, they gulped back the remainder of the wine and rushed on to the street. They watched Ronan approach.

Ronan walked past them and made his way directly into the large hall where Ivarr and his men had gathered.

"There will be sword sparks flashing now," Gorm of the Crooked Nose remarked. "Lets follow Ronan and see whats happening."

Ivarr had paced up and down the floor since he heard the news, his hands knotted behind his back. He had lost his temper.

"He is a fool, he is a fool. He will plunge the city into civil war. I should have let him die. I should never have saved him from the pens. This is the chance Sitric has been waiting for. What does Ronan know of single-handed combat. He has no experience. His sword is only a bright and ornamental toy."

Ronan came through the door and stood at the end of the hall.

"I have told them you are a fool and now I say it to your face," he roared down at him.

"You have destroyed the peace and order of the city. Why did you do it? You are my slave."

It was a brutal and angry comment for which Ivarr was immediately sorry.

"I am tired of your talk of peace, Ivarr of the Ships. I am tired of insults. I am tired of your talk. Sitric will soon rule the city. You ask why I accept the challenge? Well, I have held my tongue long enough. My sister and two brothers are in the slave pens. Soon they will be carried in captivity to the ends of the earth. If I win this fight they go free. If I lose, then I am a dead man and they go into captivity. I care now only for them."

"Leave my house. Find shelter elsewhere. You have drawn destruction upon me."

Ivarr's anger had again darkened his judgment. He had made a second mistake.

"I leave your household. For the salvation of my life I thank you. I shall return, Ivarr of the Ships, only at your invitation."

With that he turned his back upon the mute gathering.

"This Ronan has spirit," Sven of the Bent Back said following him. "Come with us Ronan. You shall stay with Gorm and the contest shall be arranged."

Astrid wept when Ivarr banished Ronan

from his house. She went to her room and locked the wooden latch upon the door. But she thought of the great fights she had seen between the hermit Aodh and Ronan as they practised in the woods. Her spirit returned. She slipped out of the house when darkness fell and made her way to the shop of the silver smith.

The tallow candles burned brightly. Ronan lay on a table and Gorm of the Crooked Nose and Sven of the Bent Back were softening his muscles with their fingers. They were so seriously engaged upon their work that they exchanged no pleasantries with Astrid.

"Take his sword and polish it," they ordered. "We have no time to waste. We have received an answer from Sitric. The contest is tomorrow at mid-day. The articles of the contest have been agreed upon. He is moving swiftly because he has his champion. The Black Warrior is ready. That is why we have to loosen Ronan's muscles. By right we would need a week. Now hurry with the sword and when you have that finished you can polish the scabbard."

Meanwhile Sitric felt confident the city of Dublin would be soon under his full command. He could banish Ivarr and Astrid.

His champion, the Black Warrior, next to Ronan was the largest man in the city. He had greater agility, and each day close to the pagan grove he kept in practice. Sitric lavished his gold upon him. He received the finest food and wine, slept in a comfortable bed and had his own quarters in Sitric's house hold. He always remained hooded and was a strange and a sinister figure.

"The boor is untested and untrained," he told Sitric as they feasted upon fine meats.

"He will be taken dead from the Pit. I shall play with him as you play a fish. Only when he is completely weakened and bleeding from many wounds will I deliver the fatal blow."

They drank deeply of the wine and retired to sleep.

In the small shop they rubbed oil upon Ronan's muscles to make them more supple.

"Keep moving your wrists and your fingers Ronan. Use the double hold and your force will be greater than his. Remember the air grows stale and warm in the Pit," they advised.

When it was darkest in the east and the west Ronan fell into a deep sleep. Astrid slipped away into the night. She would attend the fight dressed as a boy.

Next morning at early light the city stirred.

Men made their way to the Pit which was close to the slave pens. A large circular arena had been dug in the earth. On the edge of the arena were seats for five hundred men. By mid-day the seats above the Pit were crowded with soldiers and merchants who had paid a high price to watch the fight. Two platforms at opposite ends of the Pit suspended from rough frames would carry the men to the floor. Then the platforms would be quickly winched up and the Pit left empty but for the contestants. There was no door out of the Pit.

The Black Warrior was the first to arrive in armour fretted with silver. The armour had been made by the finest smiths. No one had ever looked upon face of the Black Warrior which made his appearance more sinister. He stood beside his platform and sipped a cup of wine. Sometimes in a dramatic gesture he whipped out his sword and lunged at the air with neat economic gestures.

"Ronan stands no chance against such skill," Sitric's soldiers said. "He will be soon dead."

Those seated at the top of the Pit watched the streets. They saw Ronan approach with two old men and a boy. His chest was bare and glistened with oil. His blonde hair fell on his shoulders. Ivarr was nowhere to be seen.

"The challenger comes," they called down to the others.

"Then he comes to his death," the Black Warrior cried.

Ronan came through the opening followed by the two men and the boy. He moved briskly on to the platform which stood before him. Spreading his legs he balanced on it, drew his sword and gazed at Sitric surrounded by his retinue of soldiers.

"If I live, Sitric, then the three slaves are freed. Is not that your bargain?"

"That is our bargain, fool," Sitric said dismissively. His lips were curled in disdain.

"Let us descend into the Pit then," Ronan directed.

"You wish to die early in the day," the Black Warrior called from the opposite platform.

Ronan held his concentration. The frames were swung out over the Pit. They were winched down on ship pulleys. It was a slow even descent, each man grasping his sword, his feet splayed so that he would not loose his balance.

They looked at each other. The Pit was silent. The only sounds to be heard were the sound of ropes on dry pullies and the creaking of dry frames. Ronan noticed that the air in the Pit was warm and dead. It would quickly draw away energy. Gorm of the Crooked Nose had given him a jar of honey to drink before he left the small shop. It would quickly turn to energy.

"And remember, test your opponent for two minutes. If he is expert with the sword then you must use all your strength and beat it out of his hand. You fight to the death in the Pit and there are no rules."

The platforms touch the earth. The contestants sprang forward. The platforms were quickly drawn upwards. Now the men stood alone, Ronan bare-chested, the Black Warrior carrying his rich armour. Ronan looked at the piercing blue eyes peering from the monstrous helmet. Holding their swords in front of them they moved about in a circle, stirring up the fine dry dust of the floor. They rushed furiously at each other and their swords tangled together. They tested each other's guard. The Black Warrior speedily moved back. He discovered that Ronan moved more quickly than he had been led to believe. He discovered also that Ronan was trained in the use of the sword and possessed greater strength. His mind became alert. They circled and moved together several times, then with a quick flurry the Black Warrior cut a shallow wound in Ronan's side. It crossed the old scar. Ronan felt the warm blood running down his body. The crowds were jeering. Fury began to burn within him and he thought of his brothers and sister in the slave pen. The heat was overpowering. Sweat glistened upon his body. Time was passing by. He was losing his concentration. The fight had fallen into a pattern which suited the Black Warrior. They moved about in a circle, their movements traced on the dust. They rushed together and again Ronan was lightly wounded. The Black Warrior expected him to retreat. Suddenly Ronan cried out and rushed forward. Heavy blows rained down upon him, battering at his guard. He fought back but his strength was no equal to Ronan's. He backed away but Ronan pursued him hacking from right and left, his sword glancing off helmet and armour, now a heavy burden on his opponent. Sitric cursed from his seat, calling upon him to fight back. Ronan's eyes burned with an animal fire, the fire of the berserkers. The Black Warrior thought that there must be an end to such savage blows which he continued to parry. But his strength gave out. With a swift hard side-cut the sword was swept from his hand.

"Finish him, finish him," the crowd cried with blood lust. Ronan raised the sword above him to bring it down on the helmeted head. There was fear in the blue eyes. He threw down his sword and caught the Black Warrior's helmet. He tore it from his head. The crowd gasped in surprise. His face was corrupt with disease, his head a mass of circular white scars.

"He carries the foreign pestilence," the crowd cried. "Sitric's man carries the pestilence." Ronan lifted the Black Warrior above his head and with a heave threw the figure among Sitric's men.

"Take your defeated champion with you. Two have come into the Pit and two have come out of the Pit. A curse upon your dark soul, Sitric. I have won the wager," Ronan cried.

He collected his sword and pushed it into its scabbard. Quickly they lowered the platform and hoisted Ronan up out of the Pit.

He looked at Astrid. There were tears in her eyes.

Gorm of the Broken Nose and Sven of the Bent Back jumped about with excitement, patting Ronan on the back and patting each other.

"A famous victory," they said, "a famous victory." When they controlled their excitement they looked at the wounds.

"Are they painful?" they asked.

"No," Ronan said. "They do not hurt at all."

The audience stood in awe as he passed through into the street. Sitric had withdrawn from his seat followed by his sullen men. The Black Warrior had rushed from the place covering his face with shame. He must seek out a secret place in a wood and live there.

Ronan moved quickly to the slave pen. Taking his sword he hacked down the gate. He rushed to where his brothers and sister lay tethered and cut the ropes. They threw their arms about him and wept. Later they moved away from Wood Quay and up the hill to the shop of Gorm of the Crooked Nose.

"It is a small place but you can rest here," he indicated simply.

"No they shall not," a voice said and they looked about them. Ivarr threw aside a rough cloak which he had worn to the Pit. He came forward and examined Ronan's wounds.

"They are honourable wounds. Today you have pushed back the Sitric's forces. Come with me to my house and there we will bind them. Bring your brothers and sister with you.

I have made a great mistake." They left the crowded street and entered Ivarr's house. That night they held a great feast in the Long Hall. Gorm of the Crooked Nose and Sven of the Bent Back sat beside Ivarr and Ronan. For them the times were indeed favourable. Their champion had won and they had trebled their own and the money they had borrowed. During the feast a messenger arrived from Brian Boru inviting Astrid and Ronan to his fortress by the Shannon.

Chapter Five

strid left Dublin for Kincora at the ending of summer. Ivarr printed the Christian sign on her forehead with his thumb as she prepared to leave. "Do not endanger your lives by camping in the forests. Camp only in open places and where possible find sanctuary in some monastery," he advised.

Ronan moved forward awkwardly on his horse and down the hill towards Wood Quay, followed by the Princess and his sister. Behind them rode two of Ivarr's retainers.

Ronan rode grimly and without grace. He kept to the river bank and later to the clearings. His eyes glanced uneasily from left to right as he looked for danger. No king or lord ruled in the forest. Here the brigands lay in watch from the dubious shadows.

Although Ronan was not aware of it, one of Sitric's men was already in the great forest. He met Angus of the Single eye at his cave, and gave him a small satchel of gold.

"And now you must capture Astrid for Sitric. You must hold her here in the forest. The ransom for her release will be high."

He did not tell Angus of the Single eye that Sitric intended to barter Astrid for the Nordic Crown.

Ronan as he moved along the river at a slow pace followed by Astrid, his sister, and Ivarr's men, did not know that ahead of them was danger. The forest now lay close to a river. They moved towards the narrow opening. They fell silent, and listened to the noise of harness movements. Astrid's mind became sharp. Ivarr had trained her to sense danger even as a young child. She looked at the tall trees, the dense undergrowth where danger might lie.

"I fear we are surrounded by danger, Aoife. I feel that we are riding into a trap," she said.

"What shall we do if we are attacked?" Aoife asked, sudden fear in her eyes.

"Take your horse across the river," Astrid told her.

From the dark thicket a horse whinnied.

Instantly Ronan looked in the direction from which the sound came. It lay ahead of him. Suddenly from the undergrowth five men with swords emerged on horses.

"Cross the river," Astrid cried. They turned their horses and forced them into the river which was deep and wide. Ronan struggled with his horse, grasping it about the neck as it plunged forward and began to swim. He could hear the sound of voices in his ear,

"Capture the girl on the white horse. She is the prize. Sitric will pay highly for her," they called. Ronan's horse struggled out of the water on the opposite side. He drew himself erect and looked across the river. He could not believe his eyes.

Astrid who had called the order sat calmly on her white horse. She faced the horsemen who rode towards her. The men were led by Angus of the Single Eye. His dark leather jerkin and trousers and his black horse contrasted sharply with Astrid who wore white and rode a white horse.

She held the reins firmly in her hand. She looked at the men riding towards her, certain now of her capture. She recognised the markings of Sitric upon one of the soldiers. And when she was satisfied she had drawn their attention away from Ronan and the others, with a sharp tug of the reins she turned her white horse. It whinnied with excitement and at her orders sped forward.

"What is she doing?" Ronan cried as he looked helplessly from the far bank of the river.

She had taken the horsemen by surprise. Before they realized it she was speeding down the bank of the river away from them.

"Follow her. Follow her. See how quickly she rides," Angus of the Single Eye cried.

They rode in pursuit of the figure on the white horse. Her cowl waved like a long flag in the wind. She drew it from her and let it float away. It was carried for a moment by the wind, then fell upon the ground where it was trampled on by approaching horses. The five horsemen thundered after her. She looked around her. They were advancing firmly. The space between them was growing smaller. She released the small grip she had upon the reins. Her horse, finely trained to every direction from her wrists, moved forward evenly. She caressed his white neck. She could feel the joy and exhilaration in the animal. Looking back she could see the gap between them was widening gradually. Her trained eye told her that the horses of the brigands lacked exercise. Soon the open chase would tire them but she had planned something in her mind. She changed her direction slightly, looking for the tributary they had recently crossed. She saw it some distance ahead, barely descernible running through the open plain. She spoke again to the horse and reined him a little.

"She tires," Angus of the One Eye cried.

"She tires. Forward, the prize is ours."

Just as they were gaining distance and now in full pursuit she urged her horse forward, warning him of the great leap he had to take. In front of her she now could see the tributary. She arched towards her horse's head in order to spread her weight evenly upon him. And then the bank rushed towards them. She looked down at the sullen water beneath. Then they were on firm ground again

"Oh you are the prince of horses," she cried. "You have the wings of a bird."

Her pursers rushed madly towards the stream bank. Some tried to arrest the horses by pulling sharply on the reins. They were thrown forward into the stream. Two others tried to jump to the other side. They misjudged the distance and also fell into the stream. She looked at them for a moment and laughed at the sight of them struggling in the water. She had foiled an attempt by Sitric to capture her.

Her horse was wet with sweat. Her mind began to work quickly. She remembered the directions she had been given.

Ronan had watched her move away from him in despair. Ivarr would never forgive him for being so thoughtless.

"She was foolish to part from us," Ronan told them. "We could have beaten them off from this side of the river. There is no hope for her escape."

"What shall we do?" his sister asked.

"I don't know. We cannot ride back to Dublin. It is too far. We best make our way to the monastery of Aglais and meet Brian's man. Then we can search for her although in these deep forests there is little chance of finding her."

They set out towards Aglais monastery. The forest fell away again and they were now in an open plain.

They noticed blue smoke trailing up into the sky. As they moved forward they saw the monastery built on the bend of the stream. Brian's men were waiting for them and had pitched their tents outside the monastery wall.

"Where is Astrid?" the leader asked.

"We do not know," Ronan said dully. "We were attacked from the forest and she fled. She is probably now a captive. Had the brigands attacked me in the open field then the challenge would have been equal."

"They never do. They always search for weakness and then they move. That is why they picked the place of ambush so carefully," the leader told him.

"We must move quickly down stream and see if we can discover where Astrid is hidden in the forests," Ronan said,.

"We will move out immediately although we are going into the Leinster territory."

"I care not for Maelmorda King of Leinster. The ambush happened on his territory. He is no friend of Brian's," Ronan said angrily.

"The peace is fragile and we must try and hold it," the leader said.

He ordered his men to mount their horses and move downstream into Leinster territory. Just as they had fallen into order and were prepared to march, they saw a white horse approach and a white figure on its back.

"It is Astrid," Ronan called. "She has

escaped. Brigid of Faughart has been on her side this day."

Astrid moved down the hill towards them. Ronan rushed forward to meet her.

"I feared for your life. I feared for your life," he called.

"You knew I could outride them. You know that my horse is the fastest horse in Leinster," she told him

There was very little that Ronan could say. He took the bridle of the horse and lead it down to the camp.

That evening they set out towards the Shannon. The sky was rich with colour. Astrid told Ronan of her escape and how her pursuers ended in a stream.

"I don't know whether to laugh or to cry" he said.

Later that night she heard him laughing to himself. At the end of the next day they boarded one of Brian's ships. They moved down the majestic Shannon under sail to Kincora and Brian's fort.

Chapter Six

hile Astrid sailed down the Shannon towards Kincora, Maelmorda King of Leinster was gathering the yearly tribute for Brian Boru. It was at this time of year that he was reminded that Brian was High King of Ireland and overlord of Leinster. He had greater right by blood to the title.

He watched his men bring the brown, hard hides into the courtyard of his large dun. They bound them into bundles and secured them with leather thongs. Beside the bundles of leather hides lay the softer bales of wool, shorn from the finest sheep. Together with these tributes were added a chest of gold mined in Wicklow, three tall masts cut in the forests and a herd of five hundred swine. No other leader was required to bring so many swine to Brian Boru. They were awkward, uncontrollable animals and they always drove six hundred before them, knowing that a hundred would be lost in the forests and the swamps.

"If Brian wants swine he should rear them himself," his sister Gormflaith had said in anger many times," "The tribute is an insult. "

She visited Kincora each year at the gathering of the tributes.

Maelmorda looked down from the ramparts of his dun at the six hundred confused swine beneath him. All night they would squeal and grunt, giving his household no peace. He called to his chief herdsman, "Fergus of the herds I wish to speak to you."

Fergus climbed onto the ramparts.

"Are you not pleased, King Maelmorda, at the speed with which I gathered in the swine?"

"No Fergus, but I am displeased with the swine. Take them some distance from the dun and have the young boys mount guard on them. I will not have the grunts of six hundred pigs keep both myself and the chieftains awake,"

"I will attend to it immediately King Maolmordha. We will take them to the valley where they will have sweet water."

"Whatever you wish. I'll have no pig grunt

in my dun tonight."

Towards evening the chieftains of Leinster and their clansmen began to arrive. Maelmorda, looking at them approach across the plains, knew that he could have trouble on his hands. Their allegiance to him was weak and to each other weaker still. Many times he had brought the chieftains to his dun to settle the borders of their kingdom. Each year there were skirmishes between them. They entered the dun at different intervals. They gave their horses to the attending boys, took the cups of wine offered to them and then sat about in circles each suspicious of the other.

"I see they are sullen and untrusting," he said to a captain who carried a glass of wine to him.

"And unforgiving," the captain added. "There is always the danger that they will fight among themselves. They should be unarmed as all men who enters Brian's fort at Kincora are."

"That order would be the spark to start a battle. I'd better go among them and talk to them," Maelmorda said.

He went among the tribes and gave them traditional greetings, calling out their genealogies and recalling their victorious battles.

"You greetings come cheap," O'Muireadhaigh said "and our tributes come dearly. This upstart O'Brien will have Leinster beggarded. The tributes should be coming to Naas, if we had a king who would lead us."

He had a rough troubled face and a heart filled with jealousy.

"Our time will come," Maolmorda told him. "Brian cannot live forever."

"Talk and more talk," O'Muireadhaigh said. "Our arms we should bear with us to Kincora and not the heavy weight of tribute upon our backs."

"Let us go indoors with the other chieftains, O'Muireadhaigh. There are things which one says in the open and things which should be said in secret. Brian has spies everywhere."

The advice was not lost on O'Muireadhaigh. He made rash statements in public which should have been kept for the secret councils.

Maelmorda signalled to the other chiefs and they rose from their tribal circles and entered the great hall where meats and wine had been set out. Here the men sat at a large table and food was carried to them. Soon, warm with wine, they felt less eager to open the old

wounds of war. Maelmorda called his chief
adviser Fiach. He had travelled outside the
kingdom and taken the Viking ships to
England. Maelmordha trusted the judgment
of this man above all others. He had the fine
small head of an eagle, and eyes bright with
intelligence. Better than all others, he knew
what was happening in England, the Nordic
countries and France.

"For ten years Brian had ruled peacefully.
You have borne your tributes to him and there
has been enforced peace in the land. He
smashed our power and the power of the
Norse at Glenn Mama many years ago. For
the present we must live with the memory of
that defeat," Fiach said.

"It should not have happened. We were
unlucky upon the day," O'Muireadhaigh
called out. "Had we won, a Leinster king
would be Ard Ri." Fiach noticed that he had
not mentioned the name of Maelmorda. Fiach
restrained his anger,

"I agree. But now Brian is old and no longer
has the taste for battle. The Norse, so long at
peace, are again stirred with the fever for
plunder and battle. They are despoiling the
coast towns of Britain. Through Sitric of
Dublin we have kept in contact with them. In

a major battle they would fight upon our side,"
Fiach told them.

"What shall we offer them?" a chieftain
asked.

"The spoils of Munster. The monasteries
have been well endowed by Brian. In one
stroke we can destroy Brian and Munster,
strengthen our position, make treaties with
the Norse. A King of Leinster may yet rule
Ireland."

Fiach spoke at great length and far into the
night. His voice was cold.

That night the chieftains slept in the great
hall, soldiers from each tribe guarding the
great doors.

In the morning, at early light, they set out
for Kincora carrying the tributes to Brian
Boru.

Chapter Seven

t was the time of year, with summer ending that the tributes were brought to Brian at Kincora. It was the time of year also when he renewed his friendship with Ivarr and many others and sent rich gifts in token of his affection.

The servants' gossip was carried to Lorcan, which he pieced together. In this way he had knowledge of all the undercurrents of hates and jealousies at Kincora.

"And what else have your heard today?" he asked one of the servant woman who came to see him.

"I have heard an angry argument between Gormflaith and her brother Maelmorda. She plots behind Brian's back. She has noticed how old he has got during the past year"

"And what was the cause of her anger?"

"Her brother tore the silken tunic given to him by Brian. He asked her to mend the fastening and you know what happened?"

"No. Not until you tell me," he said with irritation.

"She threw the tunic at him in rage crying out, I am not a bond woman and you are a fool. Why do your suffer this vassalage from Brian?"

"Oh she is a dangerous woman. She sows poisonous weeds among the wheat," Lorcan muttered to himself.

He decided not to carry the news of the angry outburst to Brian.

Maelmordha was smarting under the abuse he had received earlier from his sister. He paced up and down his tent. Fiach, with cold passionless eyes, sat on a chair and looked at him purging his anger with words.

"Too long we have paid the tribute. I have become his menial. I was not born to be a slave to the upstart O'Brian. What noble blood courses through their veins? How far back can they trace their geneologies?"

"Temper your angers, Maelmorda. Your time will come," Fiach told him.

"And must I continue to suffer abuse both from my sister and the O'Brians?"

"Only for a little longer."

Lorcan could sense rebellion on the summer air. He had no wish to burden Brian with his suspicions. He was an old man. Many times during the year he had expressed a wish to retire to one of the monasteries he had built and leave his kingdom to his son Murchad. Lorcan had advised him against the move. Murchad was hot-tempered and sullen. He would drive a wedge amongst all the clans. His abuse was sharpest during the tribute gathering. Surrounded by young bullies he moved about the enclosures, hurling insults at the unarmed men.

Brian had tried to train him in kingship and diplomacy. But his nature was rough and stubborn and he preferred the field of battle to the council chamber, where feuds and differences could be settled with blood.

Murchad was fanning the fire of rebellion amongst the Leinster men. They remembered each insult.

"He will bring the reign of the Dail Gash to an end," Fiach reflected.

Astrid slept in a pavilion of white silk close to the lordly river. Close by, Ronan kept guard. He was permitted to wear his large sword. Her white horse cropped grass on the

green hillside. Her days at Kincora were filled
with happiness. She rode through the oak
woods with Ronan, listening to the birdsong.
She spent a day at a convent looking at the
the manuscripts Brian had brought from
abroad and listening to the plaintive singing
of the nuns. Sometimes she visited Brian and
played chess with him.

"And tell me now about Ronan your guard?"
he often asked her.

Many times she told him how Ivarr had
rescued him from the slave pens and how he
had descended into the hell of the Pit to win
the freedom of his brothers and sisters. He
often told her of her father Ivarr who had
marshalled the Danes behind him when he
marched on Meath and wrested the high
kingship from Malachy.

"That was the great moment of unity, I
thought then that I could rule over a peaceful
country. But it was never so. Hate has always
formented in Leinster and someday there will
be a great battle."

He repeated these words many times, as if
they were preying upon his mind.

"Ivarr is correct," he told her. "He has
trading posts abroad. He has told me of
southern lands where the earth is fertile,

where the breezes are always summer breezes, where a man could be at peace. He should set out for these foreign lands."

"But he too shares your dreams. Like you he thinks that peace can be held. He has lost the wish for battle."

"Oh so have I, Astrid, but to whom can I trust my Kingdom? Certainly not to Murtagh. He would set friend against friend and cement friendship between his enemies."

Each night Brian held a banquet in the large hall. It was at such a banquet that the old grey coals of hate were blown into flame. On the walls in iron vessels tallow lights brightened the halls. The tables were laden with the finest meats in Ireland, for Brian had a high reputation for hospitality. Servant girls stood about ready to fill the goblets with mead. Beside Brian sat Astrid, Gormflaith, Brian's sons Murchad, Conchobar and Flann, Maelmorda King of Leinster and many others.

Towards the end of the feast when the noise was loud and Brian tired, Murchad ordered a chessboard to be brought and the pieces set in front of him. He challenged his cousin Conaing to a game. The challenge was accepted. Murchad hunched himself sullenly over the pieces watchful of each move. He took pride in his cunning at the game. It had the limits and the challenge of single combat on the battlefield. Soon many in the hall gathered about them. Murchad, now the centre of attention, felt confident that he could defeat his opponent. He could hear the gasps of admiration about him as he made his moves. Maelmorda stood behind Conaing's chair. He followed Conaing's moves, annoyed at many of the mistakes he was making. Had he been in his position, he could have humiliated the boastful Murtagh. Conaing made a move. He fell into Murchad's trap. It seemed the game was lost. Murchad waited for his submission.

Maelmorda, looking at the pieces, saw not only a way out of the trap but a way towards victory. He bent down and whispered in Conaing's ear. His eyes brightened. With a sudden move that only a master could have seen he moved out of danger and trapped Murchad.

Anger surged through Murchad. He quickly rose from the table and swept the pieces on to the floor with his hand.

"You are free with your advice Maelmorda. Why was not such advice given to the Norse

at Glenn Mama upon the day of your defeat?"
he cried.

"Hold your tongue," Lorcan said.

"I, the future Ard Ri, will not hold my
tongue for any scribe. The Leinster men
whisper in the enemies ear. They plot against
us. But they are woman. They fear the
battlefield where all is settled."

"You go too far," Lorcan said. "These are our
guests. They come in peace."

"They do not come in peace. I have heard of
the rumours in the settlements. My spies are
about. They say that Brian is now too old to
hold the kingship, that soon the Dal Gash will
be weak and that the young men have lost the
taste for battle, that the warriors have grown
old."

"Murchad the braggard. You will never sit
upon the throne of the Ard Ri. Your lineage is
base. No one will carry tribute to your dun,"
Maelmorda said, anger seething within him.

"The Leinster men will always drive their
swine to Murtagh. The duns of Leinster will
become piggeries," he roared.

"Hold your peace," Lorcan called.

But he would not listen to Lorcan. With
clenched fist he hit the scribe and knocked
him to the floor. Brian now moved from his

throne. He told Ronan to escort Astrid to her pavilion as he moved down to the end of the long table.

"No,"she told Ronan. "I wish to stay. I have heard of these old angers and hates. There is much news I will have to bring home to my father. I will stay."

She stood away from the group of angry chiefs and soldiers and listened to all that was said.

"You have raised your hand against a monk, Murchad," Brian said. "You bring disgrace upon my household. These men came in peace. You stir up trouble."

"There would have been no trouble if I had been permitted to lead our men into Leinster. I would have subjected them and burned their duns and taken noble hostages."

His anger was now uncontrolled. Leinster men and Munster men stood before each other in the great hall. Murchad suddenly drew a hidden dagger and would have lunged forward at Maelmorda except a swift hand grasped his wrist. Ronan, scenting the danger, had rushed forward.

The assembled men looked at the giant who had so quietly moved about Kincora during the last few days protecting Ivarr's daughter.

"Unhand me, slave," Murchad roared. "I will have your life." Ronan, grim-faced, held Murchad's hand. Then, slowly, he moved it forward until it was upon his heart. With a quick movement he could have killed him but he gave the wrist a firm twist and the dagger fell upon the table.

The action of Ronan had distracted them from their angers. "You have defiled yourself. You have hit an old monk in anger. You have proved yourself a coward and a bully," Ronan told him.

"Be at peace," Brian called to them.

"There is an end to peace and an end to tributes, Brian. We have suffered too long. We came here and offered our swords at the gates as a guarantee of peace. The peace had been broken. This very night we leave Kincora. This action of your son is the beginning of war. Return our swords and we shall depart," Maelmorda said, standing before his men.

"Slaughter then now while they are unarmed," Murchad cried.

"I will not have blood spilt in my hall," Brian said. "They came in peace. Let them return in peace."

Within the hour the Leinster men, now armed, mounted their horses, and holding torches above them moved out of the dun. Astrid watched the lights move along the bank of the Shannon. Then she saw them move across the bridge throwing long reflections on the water.

"Troubled times will flow from these events," Ronan said. "The great peace which Brian has spoken about is now only a dream. It is time to return to your father's house. News of this incident will be known in every quarter of Ireland within the next three days."

A heavy silence stood over Kincora. Old soldiers knew that soon the call would go out to join Brian's standard. This would be their last battle.

Brian Boru looked old and fragile when Astrid came to him to say goodbye.

"I have a gift for you," he said, and he handed her an ornamental box. It was Brian's chess set of silver and gold pieces.

"I cannot accept it, gracious majesty," she told him.

"Accept it. I thought I would play chess during the long days of peace. Now I have to strap on my armour and ride to battle. Carry my good wishes to your father. Tell him there is a better hope in the fertile and sunny lands of the south."

Later they boarded the long ship. Astrid and Ronan looked back at Kincora with its dun and many settlements. Slowly it disappeared. They would not visit it again.

Chapter Eight

vents now moved quickly. Stirred by anger and fury, Maelmorda called the chieftains together. Messages were dispatched through north Leinster.

Late into the nights he sat with Fiach and Gormflaith, a rough map of the territories of Ireland drawn on hide before them. Upon this map they had placed the pieces of two chess sets, representing the kings, the duns, the armies. Black marked the positions of Brian's allies, white the position of the allies of Maelmorda as well as Brian's enemies.

"Do not move directly on Brian," Fiach said. "Attack him on his flank. Attack Malachy."

Upon the large expanse of hide Malachy looked isolated. He was surrounded by enemies to the west and the south. They would cut off Brian's trade through the centre of Ireland.

Fiach, his mind moving in cold steps, toppled the dun of Malachy, then he slowly moved the white pieces into positions about Brian's territory.

"Will Brian move out of Munster?" Maelmorda asked anxiously.

"He is old now. He has lost his taste for battle. We must move rapidly," Gormflaith urged. "Winter will soon be here."

*   *   *

"You are too old to ride into battle Brian," Lorcan advised as they sat together.

"Ride I must. I cannot trust my sons."

"Send out messengers with offers of peace"

"They will not accept messengers of peace. Send for the armourer," he told a young soldier who stood guard outside his room.

"Your armour will not fit Brian. You have grown heavy," Lorcan told him. "You have remained overlord too long."

"I have listened to you during the years of peace. But now it is time for battle. Go and seek out your island in the Shannon. You will be at peace there."

"No I stay with you. I will ride beside you into battle."

"You may ride into battle at a distance. You will have much to record."

Their conversation was broken by the arrival of the armourer. Like Brian, he was also an old man. Two young men carried in the heavy pieces.

"Strap them on," Brian ordered, "and make whatever adjustments which have to be made."

They fitted on his leather jerkin, carrying the imprints of steel mesh. They could not secure it in front.

"You have not kept it supple," Brian complained. "It has gone dry."

"But we have put oil upon it each week my Lord."

"I say it is dry. Adjust the straps later. Now fit on the mail."

Brian had forgotten how heavy it was. It weighed down on his shoulders and was uncomfortable on his stomach.

"It needs to be adjusted. It needs more links. See to it immediately," he ordered.

"That is the armour of another Brian," Lorcan said when the armourer had left.

"You talk too much Lorcan. You are too

honest. Perhaps I have grown out of the armour. If I do not ride into battle then we are already beaten. Now let us talk of war."

They sat in front of the fire. They could not move in the large chess game until the opponents made their first moves.

The news of what had happened at Kincora had reached every monastery and convent.

"Is it true what we hear?" the Abbess of Inver asked the Viking Princess as she sat at table with them.

"And what did you hear?" Astrid asked

"The nobles of Leinster have withdrawn the rights of tribute. They stir up the enemies of Brian. We fear for our lives. Angry words were exchanged at Kincora. They will fan the flames of battle. We have heard that Osli, Brian's tribute collector, has already been slaughtered half a day's ride from here and the booty divided."

"And what shall you do? Have you protection?" Astrid asked.

"None but the protection of Brian," she replied.

"You must go quickly. Gather your manuscripts and treasures and hasten to Kincora."

"No, we shall stay. We have few treasures

and our dead are buried here."

Next morning they left the small convent unprotected and bounded by a bright stream. The abbess and the other nuns stood at the arched door of the chapel and waved them goodbye.

"They stand alone against the storms of war," Ronan told Astrid.

"They are poor and weak and they may survive," Astrid said as they rode on.

They kept to the open places. On the horizon they saw the black smoke from a dun rise into the sky. Later they saw in autumn silhouette horsemen lead prey and slaves across the disk of the setting sun. On the second night of their journey they camped in a hidden hollow, not daring to light a fire.

*   *   *

In the city the news that tribute had been withdrawn by The King of Leinster was the common currency of talk. The merchants, in their quarters close to Wood Quay, considered the rumours hourly. The gathering was held at the house of Ragnall of York, a Viking merchant. For three generations his family had traded between the two cities. His ships sailed northwards as far as the Firth of Clyde. His merchandise was carried overland to the Firth of Forth a journey of twenty miles. The coinage of York was in familiar use at Dublin. He was a man who did not flaunt his wealth. His money kept the sea and land routes open to him and his ships at York traded with the Baltic and the south. He was a close friend of Ivarr and if they withdrew their wealth and ships from Dublin the commerce of the city would fail.

"Are we certain of the rumours?" Ivarr asked as they sat down at his table to consider the events.

"Sitric who fears Brian has proclaimed himself King of Dublin. He has raised the taxes on us. He is no longer afraid," Ragnall of York told him

"He is a hot headed man. He fattens on rumours," Ivarr said.

"Messengers ride daily between Dublin and Naas of the Kings. It is said that Maelmordha is at present in the western part of the city," Olaf the wine merchant told them.

Ragnall of York, rolling his silver wine goblet between the palms of his hands, considered the evidence. He reflected silently for some moments. Then he spoke.

"It is obvious that something serious happened at Kincora during the tribute gatherings. The peace is broken. Sitric and Maelmorda, spurred on by Gormflaith, will now move rapidly. Unless Brian can put down this rebellion, we must move our ships and our wealth out of the city."

"Can we not offer Sitric and Maelmorda part of our wealth. Can we not buy peace?" Olaf the wine merchant asked. "Or is it time to quietly withdraw our wealth from the city?"

They were about to disband when a servant knocked at the door. Ragnall bid him enter. He whispered in Ivarr's ear.

"Thank heavens they are safe," he said. "Bid both of them enter."

Astrid, followed by Ronan, entered the large comfortable room with its warm fire, oaken beams bearing the roof and tapestries on the wall. She rushed to her father and put her arms about him.

"Now tell us all that has happened at Kincora," he said. "We are most interested."

Astrid, looking older than her fourteen years, took a seat beside her father. She placed a richly ornamented box upon the table. Then in a clear voice she told them all that passed at Kincora and what she had observed in the midlands. When she finished, Ragnall of York questioned her.

"You are certain that Brian said he must go into battle again, and that war is imminent?"

"Yes. When I said my last goodbye he gave me this gift. It is also a message."

She opened the small ornamental chest. They looked down upon the gold silver chess pieces couched in silk.

"It is his famous chess set. It is a priceless treasure. The queen's and king's eyes are of precious stones," they said in amazement.

"He said he shall not play the game of chess again," she told them solemnly.

"Then he prepares for the war and the final battle," they told her.

"Yes."

"It is now time to carry our wealth from the city," Ragnall of York told them. The meeting ended and they departed.

Sitric knew that his time had come. The old grey bearded king at Kincora, fat and gouty, would not move against them. Dublin would shake itself free of tribute. He was now king.

He made his way to the pagan grove among the marshes and there sacrificed a slave to the god Odin and prayed that his eight-footed horse would trample on his enemies.

"Odin, whose name is also fury, fill my mind with your angers. Grant me strength to bear weapons against the enemy and carry off much prey and booty. Grant Sitric, King of Dublin, victory over his enemies."

He called out his prayer in a loud voice, beating his sword upon his flat shield. His voice was carried across the marshes and lost where the sea ebbed on the sand.

As soon as he left the grove he called his men together. "Dublin is ours. No longer shall we fear the power of Brian. Muster our soldiers and unfurl our flags. Soon we shall march on Malachy and then upon Brian. We shall raise the taxes in the city. Today you shall drink the best wine. Tomorrow we prepare for battle. The power of the old king is broken."

* * *

Malachy of Meath was not prepared for the forces which now attacked his territory. He was set upon all sides. The monastery at Kells and the great book was threatened. He watched his son carried dead from the battlefield as well as many of his best warriors.

In anger he moved with his army towards Dublin. But Sitric was aware of his approach. Maelmorda's forces were brought from Leinster. They were gathered in the city for a night and looted the wine warehouses on Wood Quay. They defeated part of Malachy's forces at Howth, swung west and marched into Meath.

Ivarr watched Sitric's men pass his house, their horses laden with booty, a long line of slaves trailing behind them. Sitric would soon move against his household.

Malachy, surrounded by enemies, many of his warriors slain, the smell of burnt monasteries in his nostrils, dispatched a messenger to Brian at Kincora.

The old king decided that it was time to move.

Chapter Nine

t was late autumn. The leaves had turned brown on the trees. In the evening the sun, now bronzed like a shield, charged the Shannon and the lakes with its lustre. Thin winds set up music in the river reeds and the bees in the monastic hives were growing sleepy. The migrant geese were wheeling down from the north, black ordered shapes against the sky.

Dressed in his heavy mail, the grey beard trimmed and fire in his eyes, Brian called his chiefs to the great hall on Kincora. Some had been with him during the early days when they moved through the woods of Munster as outlaws.

"The enemy grows strong and we sit here in Kincora. Tribute from Leinster has been withdrawn and Malachy has been set upon. We must move rapidly. I give you two days to assemble your men and horses. On the third day we set out for the borders of Leinster. I will bring war into their territory."

He took his large sword and brought it down heavily on the table. "The time for merriment is over. We are now at war. Soon there will be a final battle."

The chieftains were surprised at the hardness of Brian's voice. He was no longer the old chess player who drifted into sleep as the evening came on.

Meanwhile, from all over Munster and south Connaught, the chieftains arrived with their armies. Soon the compounds were filled with soldiers who sat in groups about fires, sharpening their weapons, talking of battles they had fought, discussing the latest news carried to Kincora by the messengers.

"The Leinster men have made a mistake. They thought that Brian would not move against them," a Connaught chieftain said.

"It had to come to a battle. For too long the Leinster men have been plotting the downfall of Brian," another continued.

"The spoils of Leinster are rich. Not only are the duns filled with treasures brought from abroad through Dublin, but the gold of Wicklow flows from the mines like water from the hills."

The desire for battle grew stronger at Kincora.

Brian found a new strength surge through him. He called the chieftains to the great room and inquired about their numbers, their armour, their experience in battle. He opened the great warehouse and provisioned them with food. Night and day the blacksmiths worked in the forges. Provisions were carried to the long ships to be carried upstream and through the lakes so the horses would not be overburdened. Herbs were gathered to poultice wounds and strips of linen cut to bind them.

And then on the evening before they set out he called the chieftains together and gave them their positions on the march and in the battlefield.

Lorcan looked at Brian's face as he slept. It was creased with age and care. Time has plunged deep furrows on its surface. Then he quenched the taper and made his way to his small room.

Soon the army was provisioned and ready. Brian, anxious to set out without delay, assembled his chiefs and gave them their final orders. Certain that all was clear in their minds, the chieftains gathered their men into marching positions. They stood in long double rows each flanked by horse soldiers.

The gates of his dun were thrown open and Brian rode out flanked by his sons and chieftains. His magnificent horse, tackled in silver and fine leather, carried him to the head of the army. He raised his hand and brought it down, pointing the way towards north Leinster.

Among the reeds on the far side of the rover the spy gazed at the large army marching along the far bank. He moved quickly away as the army moved forward.

*   *   *

"Are you certain of your information?" Maelmorda asked the soldier when he reached Naas.

"I am certain. I stood by the great hall door while Brian laid out the battle plans. He will bring famine into Leinster," the soldier said.

"And you say he leads the army?" Fiach asked.

"Of that I am certain. He would not trust Murchad with so many troops."

The soldier left the great hall to Maelmorda and Fiach. There was anger in Maelmorda's eyes.

"You said that Brian was too old. You said that he would not lead his troops against me. You have made a mistake. You have not reckoned with Brian of the Hostages. He has gathered a force for a final battle. What shall we do?"

Fiach, with sharp eyes, considered the situation for a moment.

"We cannot risk a battle. If there are skirmishes they must be on the edge of our territory. And these skirmishes must carry on until the snows come. Then he will withdraw to Kincora."

"To emerge and attack again."

"But in the meantime we will have brought in allies on our sides. We will bring in forces from abroad."

These plans were considered and weighed in the presence of Gormflaith. She agreed with them. Sitric would have to be immediately informed of all which was happening.

Sitric, now proclaimed King of Dublin, grew angry when he heard that Brian intended to lead his troops into battle. "Fiach the fool has made a mistake in his judgement," he said when he heard the news. "He advised that Brian was too old for war."

Sitric grew ashen when he heard that Brian had moved across the Shannon with his troops and set up his camp on the borders of north Leinster.

"He may move directly on Dublin. The city would fall before him. What plans has Maelmorda and Gormflaith to defend me?" he whimpered to his mother.

*   *   *

Brian waited on the borders of Leinster for a challenge from Maelmorda. It never came.

"What is his game?" Murchad, anxious for battle, asked.

"He is waiting for winter," Brian said.

"The soldiers grow restless. They challenge each other to single combat. Already ten have died in this manner."

Brian considered his position. He decided to test Murchad as a leader of men.

"I have thought of the matter. The army will be divided. Half I will place under you with orders to march along the border to the south of Leinster. Wheel into the centre of the

province and march directly north. I will meet
you a month from today on the green plain of
Kilmainham before Dublin. There our forces
will unite. We will send a challenge directly to
Maelmorda."

Murchad set out. He marched his men
beyond endurance. Once they attempted to
rebel against him but he butchered the
leaders and beat the troops into subjection. He
earned the name Black Murchad from the
dunes and settlements he left charred behind
him. He gathered great booty. Yet many of his
men starved and there was no forage for the
horses. People and soldiers melted into the
landscape or hid in the woods to emerge only
when he passed. Leinster was ravaged by
Murchad. Yet he scored no victory of
importance. He burnt a black path through
the countryside and even destroyed food
which would have fed his army. As he moved
towards Dublin he was rich in booty. It was
now late November of 1013.

And then the snows came. They were
carried by hard winds. They swept in from the
north out of a grey evening. Murchad's army
woke to find the countryside a deep carpet of
treacherous snow. The path they had followed
had disappeared.

All day they moved northwards towards Dublin, men dragging their horses forward, Murchad calling to the foot-soldiers to protect the booty. The men grew weary as they dragged themselves forward, their breath fogging in the cold air. One night, when they camped beside a wood, they discovered in the morning that thieves had stolen many of the horses carrying the booty. The hoof prints were lost in the vast woods. Murchad was angry. He almost lost control of a rebellious army.

They finally dragged themselves to Kilmainham. Brian had set up his tents there. His men had brought wood into the camps and built large fires. At night the inhabitants of Dublin could see these fires burning and men walking about in front of them. Sitric looked at the distant fires. He reflected upon the fate of Dublin. Brian could have easily taken it. He was playing by the old rules of war.

When Brian saw the state of the army he had sent into Leinster under Murchad, he knew that he had made a mistake.

"He is not fit to lead an army. He is a scavenger," Lorcan said to Brian as he brought him mulled wine before he fell asleep. Brian's fingers were purple and cold as he received the warm cup into his hands.

"You are correct, Lorcan. He will not be High King when I die. Perhaps the kingship will revert to Malachy. I do not wish to talk to him. The chiefs have already told me what happened. He has razed monasteries and convents to the ground to obtain booty. I am sick at heart Lorcan. We should have gone to that island, both of us, a very long time ago."

There were tears in Brian's eyes as he spoke these words.

"I do not think I will ever have the peace I sought. Tomorrow may be my final battle."

"You have sent the challenge then to Maelmorda."

"Yes. I have sent it through Sitric."

"How long ago?"

"Three days ago. It has given us time to gather our forces on both sides."

"Will it be a bloody battle, Brian?"

"All battles are bloody. Chant some of the psalms to me. I am tired. I do not wish to think of battle."

He drank his warm wine and he listened to Lorcan chant in his gentle voice. Later he left the empty cup aside and later still he fell asleep. That night he dreamt that he had taken a small boat with Lorcan and, having said goodbye to Kincora, set off to some imagined island in the Shannon.

Next morning Brian drew up his forces into battle formation and marched them towards the walls of Dublin. There was no move from the silent city. The gates remained closed. The challenge had been given and they had not accepted it. That evening it snowed again. It fell softly and thickly. As Brian sat in his tent with his advisers he considered his position. He could have slaughtered a prey of cattle and held out for a fortnight. The men were complaining that they wished to be with their families during the Christmas-tide. He considered what he should do. Then he decided to break camp before the heavy frosts which could pin them outside the city. As Sitric watched from his tower he watched Brian's army melt into a frost haze.

"Checkmate," he said to one of his men who stood beside him.

Chapter Ten

he winter was long. The snow, now deep, was followed by hard frost which bound the landscape like iron. The ink-dark Shannon swept past Kincora. No wind stirred the frozen reeds. Heavy icicles hung from roof edges. The shy deer, driven by hunger, emerged from the bare woods and approached the settlements for food. Brian, after the long marches, seemed to grow older and more fragile. He sat for long periods before the great fire, looking at the changing flames. No messengers made their way to Kincora with news. It was a grey island in a white sea.

*　　*　　*

"Will there be a battle, Ivarr?" Astrid asked as

she looked up from the pieces on the chessboard. She broke the concentration on her father's face.

"Yes, There must now be a final battle. The rumours from the western end of the city say that Sitric at this moment is on the high seas, seeking allies," he said.

"But it is too cold to move across the seas at this time of year," Ronan added.

"Fury and anger make Sitric warm," Ivarr told them.

"And what shall do we, Ivarr, in the event of a battle?" Astrid asked.

He looked up from the pieces with his sharp blue eyes.

"What we shall do is evident. I will join with Brian in the final battle."

"And if Brian loses the battle, what shall you do then?"

"What I always have wished to do and what I should have done a long time ago — sail to the sunny lands. But let us play chess. It takes my mind from dark images."

Ronan whispered into Astrid's ear. She nodded and made her move. Ivarr looked at his silver pieces. He was trapped.

"You have won," he said smiling. "Ronan is becoming a master at chess."

"Had Maelmorda not been a great master at this game," Astrid said "then we would not have the present preparations for war."

"Wars, Astrid, have small beginnings. Let us put away Brian's golden and silver pieces. It is time for you to sleep. I have to speak with Ronan."

"Can I not sit in upon the talk?"

"Not tonight," Ivarr told her.

She rose from the table and Ivarr made the Christian sign on her forehead with his thumb. Then she went to her room. They sat in front of the large winter fire. Ivarr was thoughtful for some time, then he began to talk.

As Ivarr and Ronan sat by a fire in Dublin drinking wine at the beginning of a new year, Sitric, having endured the hardships of the seas and the biting frost, sat down to feast with Earl Sigurd of the Orkneys. Outside his long house the winds beat savagely upon the doors and roof. A whole day they had bargained together.

"You say that this Brian is old and that his territory is ill-defended," Earl Sigurd said between mouthfuls of meat.

"Yes. His kingdom is ready to fall."

The previous year Sigrud had attacked the

southern coast of Ireland and carried away booty. He wished to move south. Orkney was a bleak, exposed place. He had seen the lands of Munster from his ship. He could set up a second kingdom there and trade perhaps with the south.

"And when shall I sail to Dublin with my fleet?"

"Be there before the Christian feast of Palm Sunday," Sitric said.

"If your promises are false, Sitric, then I will feed your entrails to my ravens. Now no more talk. The New Year has been born. Let us eat and drink."

Three days without break the feast lasted. When it was finished they carried Sitric to his ship. On his journey to the Isle of Man he was sick many times. He cursed the winter feasts which lasted so long.

Brodar and his brother Ospak held joint leadership over the island. They commanded forty ships. They were dour and serious men little given to revelry. They were rivals for the kingdom of Man and suspicious of each other. Brodar had a dark mind. Once he had been a Christian but the pagan ways called to him and he fell into paganism. He was a sorcerer who called upon the dark powers of evil to direct his life. Ospak on the other hand had remained a pagan but he did not invoke the powers of evil to direct his fortune. They sat on two thrones as Sitric set out his plans.

"And what shall we gain from our services?" Brodar asked.

"Control of the eastern ports. The lands of Munster will be divided amongst you when Brian is beaten. Already we control the northern part of his kingdom."

"Rumours of war have reached us," Ospak told him. "They say that you refused to do battle with Brian."

"Such rumours are false. Ireland is now ready to rise against him. Furthermore I can promise that our kingship will be cemented by the marriage of the beautiful Gormflaith to one of you."

"Such a union would be welcome," Brodar said.

The fame and beauty of Gormflaith was widely known. Sitric was not certain if he had already promised the hand of Gormflaith in marriage to Sigurd of the Orkneys. He had made many promises in drink and even signed his name to some parchment or other. His hope was that many of them would be killed in the final battle and the promises die with them. Sitric met the lesser chiefs of the island. He promised much booty and wealth if they came and joined him. In the following weeks news would spread to the mainland ports of the impending battle. Many sea captains eager for battle would join Sitric in Dublin.

Late in January, Sitric left the island and made his way back to Dublin. He immediately informed Gormflaith and Maelmorda of all that had happened.

"When Easter Sunday comes, my brother will be King of Ireland and my son of Dublin," Gormflaith cried with joy.

*   *   *

One night, when the snow had melted in January, Ivarr and Ronan slipped out of Dublin, made their way west and forded the River Liffey up stream.

"This is the most important journey you have ever undertaken. Keep your long sword on the ready. If necessary you must die and let me escape. No man must be permitted to approach us. I can not give you further details," Ivarr told Ronan.

The moon cast a dim light on the countryside. They made their way by rough paths to the monastery at Kells.

"Who is banging upon my door?" the abbot Aidan called from within his small cell.

"Ivarr," the voice said.

"What brings you, Ivarr?" Aidan asked from within.

"The crown," he said.

There was silence for a moment.

"Has the hour arrived?" he asked.

"Yes."

Aidan opened the door and emerged from the cell. He was a thin man. His face was pinched with much fasting. By the light of the moon they made their way to the great church. Aidan lit a torch from the candle which always burned there. It cast varying shadows upon the walls and ceiling.

"Many times have we been attacked but no one dared touch the Great Book or the stone upon which it is placed," Aidan told them. They made their way up the stone church and stood before the Great Book, carrying a cover of the most precious stones.

"Its fame has travelled beyond the shores of Ireland," Ivarr said.

"I will take the book and you both will be strong enough to move the pedestal aside."

He took the precious book in his arms and

Ivarr directed Ronan to help him move aside the stone pedestal. It moved very slowly. Beneath the pedestal lay an opening.

"Bring me the torch," Ivarr directed. Ronan held the torch above the opening. Stooping down, Ivarr lifted out a square chest of oak. He placed it on the pedestal. Looking at Ronan he said: "This contains the Nordic Crown. Many say it does not exist. No man living, even myself, has looked upon it."

Even Aidan, who had complete control of his feelings, could not stifle the excitement growing within him as Ivarr broke the iron fastenings upon the box. Ivarr placed his hands gently about the crown and lifted it slowly out of the wooden chest.

It seemed to gather the light of the torch into itself. The gold rim and ribs carried clusters of precious stones. The facets caught the light, changed it into splendid colours and threw them into the darkness in warm shafts. The gold bands carried delicate scroll work beneath the precious stones, as certain and sure as the scroll work in the Great Book itself.

"It bears a script within the rim," Aidan said. They brought the torch nearer. Aidan read out the inscription.

"I, Ivarr, first Viking, am a Christian," it stated simply. "It is strange beyond words," Aidan said.

They studied the glowing crown for many minutes, their wonder growing as they examined the mastery of detail.

"It was made by a monk," Aidan observed. "It has the style of the Great Book about it."

The three figures, lit by flickering torches stayed for an hour in the church. Then Ivarr reverently replaced the Nordic Crown in the oaken chest.

Morning was breaking over the city when they unobtrusively returned.

*   *   *

Towards the end of February 1014 Ospak was certain that Brodar intended to kill him. His ambitions had grown to excess. He boasted that he would marry Gormflaith and rule the kingdom of Leinster. He promised the chiefs rich lands in Ireland. Ospak, with three ships crewed by his followers, slipped quietly away from the isle of Man as February ended. A long journey lay ahead of them. As they approached the Shannon estuary the three ships were recognized by watchmen. Quickly news was sent to Kincora of the approach of three Nordic longships. Their approach was observed. They came at an unexpected time and they flew the flag of peace. Nevertheless, Brian on receiving the news ordered his men to their ships.

The three ships offered no resistance. The men handed over their arms and their ships were moored at the piers which jutted out into the Shannon. The leader was brought to Brian.

"I am Ospak," he said directly to Brian, "I have come to join you in the final battle."

"What battle is this you speak of?"

"The battle which shall be waged during the sacred week."

"How do you know of these things?" Brian asked.

"Sitric during the darkest month made a journey to Man and other places. He has promised the spoils of Munster to those who will join him in the final battle."

"You bring strange battle news. Sit with me and tell me more."

All day Ospak sat with Brian. Towards evening Brian knew that mighty forces were ranging against him. Isolated at Kincora, his enemies were growing in strength. The Norse, anxious again for booty and new land, would do battle against him on the side of Sitric and Maelmorda. That night his sleep was troubled. He wished that winter would not pass. When the leaf was ready to open on the tree he would again have to lead his army east.

*   *   *

Astrid followed her father and Ronan down the circular stone stairs that led to the basement of the house. Very few knew of the existence of the vaulted room. A passage led from this room to the Christian church close by. Her father locked the door. Then, from beneath a slab of stone which formed part of the floor, he took an oak chest.

"Now, Astrid, I will show you the Nordic Crown. By right of blood it belongs to you."

He lifted the crown from the oaken chest and she viewed it with wonder.

"I will let you gaze upon it and then we shall hide it again. This proves that you are of royal blood for it has been passed down through the generations. I have placed it in the care of Ronan. If I should die in the coming battle, bring it with you to the Kingdom of the

Franks. I have given clear instructions to Ronan."

Astrid, heir to the Nordic Kingdom of Dublin, had no word to utter. Events were moving too quickly about her. The chest was returned to its hiding place. Then they returned to the main hall.

It was midnight in Dublin. Revellers reeled out of the taverns. Many cried out their allegence to Sitric. The loyalties of the city were divided unequally.

Chapter Eleven

n early April leaves were opening on the trees. Tomar's Wood near Clontarf was touched with soft green. The days were clear and from the ramparts of the city Gorm of the Crooked Nose could see the smoke arising from the settlements at Howth and the fishing villages close to the long Clontarf strand.

"Soon I will go south and fish in the clear streams," he told his friend Sven of the Bent Back as they looked northwards to the green plains. "This may not be a year for fishing. Look at the river. More strange ships arrived this morning. They are no traders. They bear arms. In drink they boast of killing the old King of Munster."

"This may be the year for fishing. I have no taste for blood. There is peace in the greenwood and nobody robs a poor man,"

Curiosity drew them towards Wood Quay. They counted the foreign ships moored to the wooden piers. They now amounted to one hundred.

"The river will be choked with ships," Gorm of the Crooked Nose said "I have never felt such a fever for battle".

The streets were crowded with foreign Norse. They stood about the slave pens peering at the slaves or made their way to the markets where they examined goods brought from foreign lands. But most of all they frequented Wine Tavern Street. Even at mid-day they fought in the open street.

Having walked through the city, Gorm of the Crooked Nose said to his friend, "I think that you should come fishing with me."

"No. I will remain here. There will be much to see and I shall tell you all that happened when you return."

What was obvious to Gorm of the Crooked Nose and his friend was more obvious to Ivarr. He had counted the ships and knew their ports of origin. Rumours of booty and wide lands had travelled widely during the month of March. The merchants had already removed their gold and precious stones from the city. He wondered if he should quickly gather his soldiers and move west to Kincora and join Brian there. But prudence told him not to leave the city. There was always the fear that Sitric might make a sudden move against his household. He travelled through the city in disguise, entering the taverns and listening to the loose tongues of the foreigners.

Meanwhile at Kincora Brian was aware that the Norse were gathering in the city. He knew the names of many of the leaders.

"By Easter Sunday the final battle will have been fought," he told Lorcan.

"And will you lead the army?" Lorcan asked.

"Yes. Malachy of Meath and the men from Connaught will march with me. We will out-number our enemies."

As the Norse forces were gathering in Dublin, Brian provisioned for a month, set out from Kincora. He moved along the northern border of Leinster and ordered part of his army into south Leinster under his son Donnchad. As Brian moved forward he was joined by chieftains from Connaught.

Brian took a keen interest in the countryside. He had moved across it many times during his life and he knew its rivers and woods. The fresh sap was strong in blade and branch, and the morning air fresh. Winter which had chained his body and his mind had passed to the north. Day and night messengers arrived at his camp bearing tidings from Dublin and Meath. He knew that the river Liffey was crowded with ships and that in Leinster the army of Mealmorda was assembling at his great dun.

Brian intended to reach the plains of Dublin at the beginning of Easter Week. He had wished to celebrated the feast of Easter at Killaloe but his wish would not be granted.

Maelmorda gathered his forces. They were eager for the coming battle. They would no longer carry tribute of Brian and they would make Black Murchad pay for wasting Leinster. News that the Norse were crossing the seas to join Sitric gave them heart. Gormflaith joined her brother and Fiach to plan the battle moves. There could be no turning from this engagement. Her happiness or despair depended upon the outcome.

In Dublin Sitric marked the approach of the Norse ships. Earl Sigurd of the Orkneys arrived with fifty ships. Later Brodar arrived with his fleet. Many adventurers who had heard promise of booty and plunder arrived at the port.

But he was also aware that many of the merchants had, under the cover of darkness, sailed out of the port with their gold and valuables. He should have moved upon them. Their gold would have provided money to pay his army. He had to billet the foreigners and feast their chiefs. During one of the feasts news was carried to him that Brian had plundered north Leinster, crossed the Liffey and was marching towards the open meadows of Kilmainham. Next morning he rode across the city and mounting the Western Tower looked towards the meadows. His eyes caught the forms of soldiers approaching. They marched under standards. Finally he made out the figure of his hated enemy, Brian of the Tributes.

"Who leads the army?" Brodar, who had now joined him, asked.

"Brian of the Tributes," he replied, a cold sweat breaking out on his forehead.

"So this is the ailing king you spoke about," Brodar remarked sharply.

"He is old but he is not ailing," Sitric answered, quibbling with words.

"You have lied to me Sitric. I thought we would march on his kingdom. He carries his challenge to the very walls of your city."

As they watched in awe, the army of Brian approached along the northern band of the river. It marched under careful discipline.

"These soldiers are battle trained. They had been in the field before," Brodar told him angrily.

Now their eyes were drawn towards the north. An army approached from that direction.

"Who comes to join Brian?" Brodar asked.

"Malachy of Meath," Sitric replied, fear edging his voice.

"Then we have two armies to fight. You have played me false Sitric."

"You wish for booty and the lands of Munster. Then you must fight for them. If they were easy picking I would not have asked you for help," Sitric answered acidly.

Quickly news that Brian had arrived at the very gates of Dublin spread through the city. Soldiers issued from taverns and rushed to the ramparts. The size of the double army made them sober. They gazed at the figure of Brian. He was the leader who had never lost a battle. He sat firmly on his horse and looked towards the ships, the quays, and beyond that to the ramparts. Taking the banner of challenge he planted it firmly on the ground.

The first move in the chess game of battle had been made. The challenge was given on Wednesday of Holy Week.

Having placed the challenge he ordered his army away. They moved to the middle distance not far from Tomar's Wood. To the east lay the long flat strand of Clontarf.

*   *   *

"What move shall we make?" Earl Sigurd of the Orkneys asked at the council of war which was quickly drawn up.

"His army if too large. It is battle-trained. I shall take my ships and return to Man. The Leinster army has not arrived and the city and the ships are in danger," Brodar told them.

"Then you fear death," Sitric said tauntingly.

"No I do not fear death but I am not a fool. The armies are not evenly matched."

Sitric looked at the faces about the hall. They had seen the army of Brian. They were experienced warriors and warlords. The odds lay against them.

"I agree with Brodar," Sigurd of the Orkneys said, "The odds are too high."

Sitric felt anxious. He would be banished from Dublin. Exile would be bitter to him. While he stood in the great hall, waiting for the leaders to disperse, news was brought to him of Maelmorda's approach with the Leinster army.

"Now both sides are equal," Sitric told them. "Did I not tell you that an army would march from Leinster."

The army reached the city at mid-day. They carried battle fever with them.

"We shall sacrifice a sheep to Thor. Brodar is a seer and can tell us the outcome of the battle," Sitric told the chieftains.

"Very well," they said. "We will go to the grove and sacrifice a sheep to Thor and Brodar will read the message in the entrails."

*   *   *

In the household of Ivarr, the news of Brian's arrival on the plains beyond the river was greeted with relief. He was no longer isolated within the city. Now he must put his affairs in order.

If Brian were defeated than he would quickly have to leave the city. If he were victorious then his position would be made strong.

The night of Brian's arrival before the city he bid Ronan to sit with him.

"The forthcoming battle will be long and bloody. I will join Brian. We have fought together before. You must stay in this house. I have ordered the ships to anchor at Howth. If we are defeated than bring Astrid and the Nordic Crown to the ships.

Ronan made a firm promise to follow the orders.

"Now we must sleep. Thursday will be a busy day."

On Thursday morning Malachy and Murchad moved towards Howth. They wished to protect the left flank of the army from sudden attack. They put all the settlements in the area to the torch. The inhabitants and soldiers were scattered. From the ramparts, Maelmorda and Sitric watched the smoke rise towards the sky.

"Brian has made his first move," Maelmorda said, fury rising within him. "He tempts us into the fields."

"Soon he will make a move upon the city. The bridge is heavily defended and can be quickly destroyed," Sitric added.

The Norse were not anxious to join in the

battle. They sat in the alehouses and drank beer. They considered their dubious position. But that evening news arrived from Brian's camp which made them change their minds. The odds were now in their favour.

*   *   *

As Murchad and Malachy returned to Brian's camp with their booty, a dispute broke out among the soldiers.

"Malachy did the looting while Murchad did the fighting," the followers of Murchad said.

"Malachy never shirked a battle," came the reply.

"When he smells danger he turns on his heels. We cannot depend upon him in battle," Murchad added.

His voice was loud and angry. Men began to draw their swords.

"Put away your swords," Malachy told his men. "Murchad, the fool, has a loose tongue. It was his loose tongue at Kincora which has drawn the present events upon us."

"You insult me, old man," Murchad cried.

"I tell you the truth. You boast that you will be King of Ireland. I would have a Viking crowned at Tara before I would submit to a fool."

Malachy could not control his anger. Murchad drew his sword and brought it flatly down on his helmet. Malachy lost his balance and fell from his horse. Murchad and his chiefs laughed at his misfortune.

"We need no Malachy in the final battle," Murchad called out boastfully.

"Then you shall not have him," Malachy said, rising from the ground. He mounted his horse and ordered his troops to march northwards towards Meath. Brian had lost his finest ally.

Brian told his men to leave the tent when the news was brought to him. He had a heavy decision to make. Should he retreat or should he do battle next day.

"It would be cowardice to retreat, Lorcan. To attack with our present strength would be folly. If I retreat then Sitric and Maelmorda will crow at our departure. They will march upon our kingdom. What shall I do?"

"I know nothing of these matters," Lorcan said. "But if you retreat then many will rise against you. If you are defeated they will also rise against you."

"There is balance and wisdom in what you say. I will order the men to prepare for an immediate battle."

The chieftains were called. They filed into the tent and stood about him. He told them that on the next day, Good Friday, they would engage in battle against the enemy. He gave them their positions, then bade them depart and prepare their troops.

*　　*　　*

It was the news of Malachy's departure which destroyed any doubt that Earl Sigurd and Brodar might still have entertained concerning the outcome of the battle. Word quickly passed through Dublin that the Norse chiefs had decided to engage Brian. That night soldiers pledged friendship to each other in the ale houses. More cautious soldiers sharpened their weapons and felt battle anxiety and fear in their hearts. They invoked the dark gods to take their parts.

Ivarr, with a hundred men, slipped out of the city, crossed the river and made his way into Brian's camp.

In Sitric's long hall the chieftains set out their battle positions. They would fight with their backs to the sea. The morning light would give them an advantage. On their left flanks would be positioned their ships, safe and secure for a sea retreat. Sitric would remain in Dublin to protect the city from attack.

In serious mood they retired to sleep.

Chapter Twelve

n the half light men began to stir. The trampled grass was grey with dew. The small wind had the sharpness of frost in it. It stung men's senses. They became quickly awake. They took oaten bread from their satchels, broke it between their hands and munched at it thoughtfully. Their minds were on the battle. The gillies sought the horses cropping in the wide meadows to the west of the camp. They brought them into the circle of tents and spoke softly to them as they dried the night damp from their flanks. The tents and sleeping quarters covered many acres of meadow.

Soon the fires were alight, the oak-scented smoke carried towards Howth. As the light hardened the noise about the tents grew louder, the movements more hurried. Some of the chieftains drank cups of warm mead brought to them by their gillies. The common soldier drank warm milk. Many nervously, and in silence, polished and repolished their swords. There was the jangle of horse tackle and mail.

They all looked towards the gate at Dubgall's Bridge. This was the bridge which would carry the enemy across the river and on to the field of battle. On Clontarf strand the tide was beginning to rise. A few Norse ships had lifted their anchors and moved towards Clontarf island. Two crew members manned each ship. Brian's horse soldiers, on the move since early dawn, carried this news to the camp.

A horn sounded. The soldiers began to move towards their sections. The horses whinneyed as they were brought into battle formation. Behind the horses the soldiers took their places. Murchad, his anger now turned to battle fury, would lead the southern flank of the army. He could cut off the retreat towards Dublin.

"Once over Dubhgall's Bridge," he declared, "there will be no returning for the Leinster men."

The heaviest fighting would take place on

Murchad's flank. His son was given charge of the central army and the north flank was led by the Connaught leader, Aidne.

"The sea will be their greatest enemy," Brian told his chieftains in the tent before the battle. "If we retreat, we have an advantage. They have none. They must always press forwards. Guard all the wells. Men cannot drink sea water."

*   *   *

He gave them his final orders. When the army was in battle order he mounted his white charger and moved down the ranks, his keen eye searching for weakness. Men lifted their swords and cheered him. Then he returned to his tent by Tomar's Wood. Ten men stood about it ready to defend him with their lives.

And soon the gate of Dubhgall's Bridge was opened and the army of the enemy began to march across. Murchad watched the almost endless line of men and horses emerge from the gates and move across the plain which led down to the sea.

They moved into battle formation, their backs to the light and to the sea. Behind them the tide continued to rise. Soon the chess pieces were set upon the field of battle. A horn sounded three times. It re-echoed off the ramparts of Dublin and rolled across the wide space dividing the two armies. Then the final sound died. The voices of ten thousand men filled the air. The armies moved towards one another at an even pace. They did not break their ranks. The green space between them grew narrow. Soon their battle cries mingled. They could make out individual horsemen and soldiers. Each wondered how many men would die on that day. They could now hear the noise of each other's armour and horse tacklings. They could make out the faces of their enemies, grim, fierce, clear-eyed. They rushed forward. There was no gap between them. Men, swords, horses tangled in battle confusion. The battle of Clontarf had begun. The tide was full.

*   *   *

. . . For Sitric there was much to be done. News had come to him that Ivarr and his men were fighting on the battlefield beyond the river. His house was undefended but for the giant soldier Ronan. He would make Odin a sacrifice which would satisfy him. He would slaughter Astrid in the pagan grove. Such young and royal blood would buy him the favour of the gods. He would destroy his rival claimant to the throne.

He summoned his men. Unchallenged, they swept across the city. From his shop, Sven of the Bent Back looked at the men driving their horses up the hill towards Ivarr's house. He watched them beat upon the door. An old servant who opened the door was cut down. Horses neighed and shied in confusion. They might have dismounted and entered the house but Ronan emerged with sword drawn. They drew back in fear for a moment. Then they moved into a half circle about him. He stood with his back to the wall. They forced the horses upon him. He cut at their necks. Blood spouted on to his hands and two horses fell at his feet. Men fled between the small streets. Other horsemen advanced upon him but strength surged through his body. He hacked at the forms of man and animal, caring little for sword skill. And then he heard the sound of Sitric.

"Hold him off, men. We have captured Astrid. The prize is ours. Sitric will soon be the only heir to the throne of Dublin."

Ronan, surrounded by dead horses and men

and with blood thickening on his hands and arms, cried out, "All is lost. All is lost. I have betrayed my trust."

Sven of the Bent Back gazed through the window at Ronan. He emerged from his house when the enemy had disappeared.

"An outrage in the city and a battle on the plains of Clontarf," he said to himself. "Clearly the whole world is in confusion,"

He looked at the half circle of dead horses and men and then at Ronan, his hands and sword sticky with blood.

"Perhaps all is not lost," a voice said. Ronan and Sven of the Bent Back looked towards the narrow street. A huge dark figure emerged. His head was covered with a hood and they could only see the eyes and the mouth.

"Who are you?" Ronan asked the mysterious figure.

"I am the Black Warrior. I have been to the hermit Aodh in the southern woods. He has given me herbs and ointment for my disease. It has been arrested but no one must look upon my face again. I owe you my life Ronan."

Ronan recollected their savage battle in the pit.

'All is lost. No one knows his way through the west of the city." Ronan said.

"None but the Black Warrior."

"We are out-numbered," Ronan told him.

"We must move quickly. Sitric intends to sacrifice Astrid to Odin. He believes her young and royal blood will buy favour with the god."

"I will carry with us a prize to tempt Sitric," Ronan told him.

"What prize?"

"The Nordic Crown."

"Do you think it exists?"

"Come with me," Ronan directed to the Black Warrior and Sven of the Bent Back. He brought them to the cellar where the chest had been hidden. He took it from a wall, opened the lid and showed them the treasure. They gazed in wonder at the crown. When they held it in the open light it cast off a thousand colours. Sven of the Bent Back was dry of tongue.

"May I touch it?" he asked.

"You can carry it," the Black Warrior said, "for you are coming with us to the eastern part of the city."

"I have no taste for excitement. I fought all my battles a long time ago," Sven of the Bent Back said.

"I'll cut out your prattling tongue if I hear another word from you," the Black Warrior said.

"I'll need protection."

"You'll get it. You ride behind Ronan."

They brought two horses from the stables and with Sven of the Bent Back clutching on to Ronan's belt and the Nordic Crown in a cloth bag, clutched to his chest, the two horses sped towards Sitric's quarter.

Meanwhile, on the wide plain of Clontarf, the battle continued. The lines held. Sometimes Brian's army pushed the enemy towards the sea; at other times it appeared that the enemy would break through and encircle them. The battle was fought with fury. The dead were trampled under foot by the living as they moved against their enemies. The dead on either side were of equal number. Many, maimed and wounded, tried to drag themselves from the field. But they were set upon, their plea for mercy stifled by a sharp sword stroke.

The sun warmed the long line of fighting men. The drunk heavily from the leather bottles they carried by their sides. But Brian's army held the wells. Many times his soldiers rushed to the water sources, cupping water over their bodies with their hands, drinking deep of its coolness, then rushing back to battle.

Murchad, in command of the southern flank, had by mid-day engaged in two single combats. Two of Sigurd's chieftains offered him challenge. Their deaths came quickly. Murchad attacked with fury, bearing heavily down on each chieftain, plunging his sword through the coats of mail. But he also kept a firm eye on all that was happening about him. The seasoned soldiers under his command knew that they had to swing down behind Sigurd's troops and cut off their retreat to Dublin. All through the mid-day while the tide was falling they wheeled the enemy away from the city.

In the tent, beside Tomar's Wood, Brian listened to the fury of the battle. Messengers came to him from all parts of the battle field. At mid-day the outcome was uncertain.

"If I had Malachy's men to throw into the centre we could break them," he told Lorcan.

Anxiously he followed the tides of battle, each moment expecting his army to break under the strain. Murchad, upon whose judgement victory rested, was pushing Sigurd's men away from Dubgall's Bridge. Brian sensed that victory might yet be his. He would win the final battle.

The tide had now ebbed. The flat sandy beach of Clontarf, neatly ribbed, was drying under the sun. Many of the Norse were growing thirsty. They retreated to the shore in search of water. It was nowhere to be found. Their mouths were dry, their tongues hard as leather. They returned to the battle, thirst now beginning to burn within them. They must have water. Many took the water bags from the dead and drank the contents. The wells were behind Brian's lines. They must break through to them. As the sun passed across the sky the battle dead became more numerous. They marked the space across which the waves of battle had passed during the day. Men were growing weary. Their arms ached. Lifting either axe or sword became painful. The battle should have long since been decided. With men so evenly matched it would never end. The tide had turned and was now washing back over the dried sand.

*   *   *

Sven of the Bent Back held firmly to Ronan's belt. Sometimes he bent out from behind Ronan's back and looked forward. The narrow alleys and roads were deserted. The inhabitants of the city were on the ramparts of the city looking at the progression of the battle. Sven of the Bent Back was confused. He had lost his bearings. He hoped that he would not have to make his own way home. Over the roofs of the houses came the din of distant battle. He thought of his friend Gorm of the Crooked Nose fishing on the bank of some quiet river.

"We ride to our deaths, Ronan," Sven of the Bent Back said when they entered the quarter of Sitric.

"Quiet. Keep your eyes peeled for enemies."

"I cannot look through your back."

"Well look to the side. Look down the alleyways."

He did.

"Quick Ronan, to your left," he called. Two of Sitric's men rushed at them. With a quick side-sweep Ronan cut at them. Wounded and crying with pain, they disappeared. He would have much to tell his friend if he ever lived, something he now doubted.

News must have reached the fortress of Sitric that they were approaching. Eight men stood as a challenge at the great door. The Black Warrior charged forward followed by Ronan. The force of the charge carried them through the soldiers and into the compound. Quickly they dismounted. Standing back to back, Ronan and the Black Warrior waited for the soldiers. They formed into a circle about them. They moved inwards and engaged in battle. The outcome was quick and decided. Six of Sitric's men lay dead at their feet. The rest fled. The Black Warrior grabbed a wounded soldier and held a dagger to his throat.

"Where is Sitric and Astrid?" he asked drawing blood.

"It is too late. He has taken her to the island with some soldiers. He is to sacrifice her to the god Odin."

"Then we must move quickly," the Black Warrior said. They mounted their horses and rode to the edge of the marshes.

Astrid looked up from the bottom of the boat at Sitric. There was a white madness in his eyes. She was so filled with fear that she could not cry out. She knew that the boat was passing through the marshes. Singular branches passed above her. She prayed to the Christian God to protect her from her enemy.

They beached the boat on an island. Roughly they bundled her on to the shore. It was an evil place. The stench of decaying animal bodies filled her nostrils. They dragged her along a pathway to the rough temple from whose beams hung the remains of sacrificed animals. The altar was black with blood.

"And now you may cry in vain. The din of battle will stifle your agony. The noble house of Ivarr will be no more," Sitric cried with joy. "Bind her and place her upon the altar. When the sun is at it's highest she will die."

Bound hand and foot, her mouth stopped by a rough cloth, she lay upon the altar. Sitric and his men watched the passage of the sun up the sky.

* * *

Ronan, The Black Warrior and Sven of the Bent Back made their way through the city to the edge of the marshes. A small thatched cabin stood beside a rough jetty.

"Bring us to the island of sacrifice," the Black Warrior ordered the old ferry-man who guarded the boats.

"It is more than my life is worth, soldier," the ferry-man told him.

"Then you die here or the islands," the Black Warrior told him drawing his dagger.

"I die here. I will not row to the Sanctuary of Odin."

Looking at the fear in his eyes the Black Warrior sheathed his dagger.

"Then give us directions to the island."

Having received directions they pushed off from the shore in a timber boat. The islands and the mid flats were a tangled mystery. As they rowed forward through the islands Ronan called out.

"Sitric, I carry the Nordic Crown with me. The life of Astrid for the Nordic Crown."

His voice re-echoed through the islands, covered in shrub and bush.

They looked to the left and the right They could not discover the island described by the ferryman. Ronan continued to call out, and then from the shore of a densely covered island they heard the voice of Sitric.

"Let me see the Nordic Crown."

They looked in the direction of one of the islands. They saw Sitric and his men emerge from the cover of trees.

Ronan took the leather bag from Sven of the Bent Back, opened and held the crown aloft.

"Come closer," Sitric ordered.

"No, if we deal we deal here in mid-stream. Bring Astrid with you."

"How do you know that it is a genuine crown."

"The name of the first Ivarr is inscribed upon it."

"I will come and examine it," he said.

"Bring only two of your men." the Black Warrior told him.

On the altar Astrid could hear the voice of Ronan carried faintly through the trees.

Ronan watched Sitric enter the boat with two of his men. He held the Nordic Crown aloft. Sitric, his eyes never leaving the jewelled crown, was lured towards it as a moth to a candle. And then he was close to the boat.

"Can I touch it?" he asked.

"You may," said the Black Warrior.

The oarsman brought the boats together. Sitric held out his hands to touch the precious object. As he did the Black Warrior jumped from the boat. It rocked for a moment and when it was stable the Black Warrior had his dagger at Sitric's throat.

"That was not the bargain," Ronan said.

"Neither was it the bargain to hide spearmen in the island beside us. We would have been killed as soon as we give him the crown. Call off your men or you will be less an ear," the Black Warrior told him.

He called off his men. As Ronan looked he
say men withdraw from hidden positions in
the island beside him.

"Now have Astrid brought to us or you shall
die" he ordered.

Sitric's eyes wide with terror called orders
to his men. Very soon Astrid was brought to
them. Ronan helped her into the boat.

"It was horrible, horrible," she kept crying
as Ronan put his arms about her. "I hate this
paganism of Sitric."

"Do not fear. Do not fear. All will be well."

When the Black Warrior was satisfied that
they were free of danger he ordered the
oarsmen to swim ashore. Then he removed
Sitric to their boat and set the other adrift.

"If they follow, you die," he told Sitric.

As they made their way through the marsh
islands towards safety Astrid asked to see the
crown. She took it in her hands and said "I
have been brought safely through terrible
danger. If my father's life is spared then the
gold of this crown will be melted and made
into a sacred vessel. The jewels and precious
stones will be set in a reliquary. I have no
desire to be queen of a slave city."

"Never," Sitric cried. "Never. It is a waste."

"I have made the promise and I will keep it.'

The rest of the journey was made in silence. In all his days Sven of the Bent Back had not lived so dangerously. He would have much to tell to Gorm of the Crooked Nose during times of peace.

*   *   *

On Clontarf Strand the tide was filling. All day the battle had raged. It had moved in many directions. But now the southern flank under Sigurd was bending away from the city. Aidne was also pressing forward. The Leinster army had lost Maelmorda. Men cried for water and fought their way towards the wells. Now all the wells were blooded. Murchad cried for drink but none was to be had.

Towards evening and weary, he faced Sigurd in single combat. It was a raw unskilled battle as they hacked at each others guard. Murchad in one savage attack lost his weapon. Empty handed he attacked Sigurd. A blow fell on his arm piercing the mail. The wound set fire to his fury. He grabbed Sigurd, wrenched the sword from his hand and cast it aside. Then he ripped open his mail and plunged a dagger into Sigurd's chest. Sigurd cried out that he was dying. As Murchad drew away from him Sigurd in a final gesture thrust his dagger into Murchad's ribs. He began to die. He would not die easily. He would be carried to his tent, survive the night, and having received Viaticum on Saturday, die.

Murtagh, standing upright, ordered his men forward. News quickly spread that Sigurd was dead. The heavy southern flank of his army began to weaken. Men threw down their weapons and fled towards the oncoming tide. Safety now lay in the sea and in the long boats. Soon the enemy line began to collapse. A cry of victory rose from Brian's forces. They surged forward. Victory was theirs. It had been their longest battle. It lasted from high tide to high tide.

Brodar on his right flank gathered some of his followers about him. He would break out of the trap and make his way towards Finglas. Ivarr, fighting in the central section watched the small band of Norse escape from the trap. He called his men to follow him.

Brian had sat all day in his tent. Lorcan had stood beside him. He had followed the events of the battle. Many of the O'Brien princes had died during the day. Many of the old veterans who had been with him in the early campaigns were also dead. His heart was heavy. He heard the guards about the tent call out.

"Victory is ours. The enemy are in retreat towards the sea."

Blood lust gripped them and many rushed into the battle.

Brodar recognized that the tent with Brian's ensign flying above it. He gathered his men about him. They would sweeten defeat. They bore down upon the few remaining guards. It was a short combat.

"I hear Norse voices," Brian told Lorcan.

Lorcan scarcely reached the tent opening. He cried out to Brian as the sword entered his chest. Brian looked up. The blow came suddenly.

Drawing the sword from Brian's body, Brodar cried, "Now soldier can tell soldier that Brodar slew Brian."

*   *   *

Ivarr realized that he was too late. He entered the tent and looked at the body of his old friend. The crown had rolled from his head. He noticed its imprint on his grey hair.

"You lost and you won, Brian. All your battles are now over," he said, and bending down beside his friend he wept.

Brodar died later in Tomar's Wood. Had he not stopped at Brian's tent to vent his revenge he would have lived.

As the sun began to settle Ivarr took stock of the battle-field. Many corpses lay on the wet strand. On the plains of Clontarf the wounded were helped away. The dead would be buried on the field. The Norse power had been broken. The Leinster army was in disarray. The Munster army had been weakened. It must now make its long journey back to Clare. Brian, with his dead sons and in accord with his wishes, would lie beside Patrick in Armagh.

It was time for Ivarr to sail towards the south.

EPILOGUE

t was Holy Saturday. There was a heavy silence over Clontarf. The dead were buried on the stained field. In the east the shore sand was blood clean. The remnants of Brian's army gathered about their tents or sat, their backs hooped in fatigue, over their camp fires. The body of Brian, Emperor of the Irish, lay upon a bier. It would soon be carried to Armagh. All the leaders had been slain.

Ivarr remained on the battle-field during the night. He awaited news from the city. Sitric had not been on the field of battle. He wondered what treacherous moves he might have made during his absence.

And then from the west he noted the approach of four riders. He recognized Astrid and the figure of Ronan. The other two he did not immediately know. As they approached he saw a head peering from behind Ronan's back. It was Sven of the Bent Back. Ivarr wondered how he had become caught up in the affairs of war. As they approached nearer he recognized the figure of Sitric bound upon one of the horses. The reins were held by the sinister figure of the Black Knight.

Ivarr rushed to the white horse and swept his daughter from the saddle.

"You are safe, father," she cried

"Yes, I am safe, but Brian is dead. We have won the battle and lost it. Murchad too is slain and so is his son and many other chieftains. There is no power now to bind the clans. But what of you. You look troubled?"

She was not given time to answer. The Black Warrior in a deep voice told Ivarr what had happened.

"Sitric would have done her to death on the altar on Odin's island had we not arrived with the Nordic Crown. He does not deserve to live."

He drew his heavy sword and would have brought it down upon Sitric's head but Ivarr restrained him with a gesture.

"Stay your hand. I have seen enough of blood. Let Sitric look upon the field of battle and contemplate what he has brought about. Let him then gaze upon the city he has destroyed by his ambition. The merchants and the sea captains have left it. Soon I will depart."

"Then you wish to let him go free," the Black Warrior said.

"Yes. That is my wish."

The Black Warrior released the horse and brought his sword down on its back. It carried Sitric towards the city.

"And how did you get drawn into all this Sven?" Ivarr asked.

"It is a very long story, Ivarr. A very long story."

"Then keep it for Gorm of the Crooked Nose when he returns from his fishing. But let Ronan tell us the story briefly."

When Ronan was finished, Astrid told him of her promise.

"It is your crown, Astrid, to do with it whatever you wish. If it is your desire then the gold will be made into a sacred vessel and the jewels and precious stones placed on a reliquary."

"That is my wish, but now I must go and pray over the body of my friend Brian."

Mounted upon her white horse she rode

through the long straggling camp. Men, still fatigued by battle, looked at her with dull eyes. She passed the wounded crying out for water. Rough bandages bound their heads and their limbs.

"Perhaps in the southern lands there will be no more war," she thought as she looked at the horrors of battle.

She stopped in front of Brian's tent now guarded by twenty soldiers. She dismounted and entered. A great purple cloak with gold fastenings was gathered about Brian's body. The wound on the side of the head was wet and grey. The clotted blood had been washed away. She looked at the hands. They were long and fine. She recalled how neatly he moved the chess pieces about the board at Kincora. She wept openly. Later she left the tent.

That night Ivarr and the others returned to Dublin. It was a time for leave-takings. Ivarr's ships were at anchor beyond Clontarf. They would take his household and his followers south. Astrid visited her friends in Winetavern Street and Wood Quay. They had watched her grow in stature and in beauty. She was taking leave of her childhood and her youth.

"Some day I shall return and visit you all again," she promised. But they knew that she would never return.

Easter Sunday brightened on the eastern sky in white silver. The world was sharp and clear, the sky cloudless.

Ivarr mounted his horse. Beside him were Ronan, Astrid and the Black Warrior, behind him his followers.

They moved out of the city in the early light. They crossed the Liffey and made their way to the field of battle. The soldiers were preparing to carry the body of Brian to Clontarf. Ivarr and his men joined the cortège. They followed the body of their friend in a slow funeral procession to Swords. Then Ivarr directed them to break away.

The three ships were waiting to bear them south. They were provisioned for a long journey. Soon they were all aboard, except Ivarr, Ronan, the Black Warrior, Sven of the Bent Back and Astrid.

"Will you come with us, Ronan?" Astrid pleaded when the moment came for them to depart.

"No I shall remain with the Black Warrior. I am not a sea traveller."

"Then ride with us to the ships," Astrid

begged.

Ronan, the Black Warrior and Sven of the Bent Back followed Astrid and Ivarr into the water. The waves passed evenly by them. When Astrid was safely on board she said to Sven of the Bent Back, "Keep my horse, Sven, and take good care of him."

"I will. I will," he said weeping.

Ivarr clasped Ronan's hand and then that of the Black Warrior. He patted Sven of the Bent Back on the head and told him to take care of his friend.

"Goodbye, Astrid," the three said finally. "And fair luck go with you." They turned their horses and moved shorewards.

When they reached the shore they looked towards the sea. The sails had been raised. The ships were moving towards Ireland's Eye. It was Easter Sunday and the wind was fair. It was the day of the Resurrection, the best of days to travel south.